Sandra E Sinclair
Pastor's
Heart

PASTOR'S HEART

Oakbrook Faithful Heart Series – Book 1
Christian Romance Series

Sandra E. Sinclair

This book is a work of fiction. While reference might be made to actual historical events or existing locations, the names, characters, places, and incidents are either the product of the author's imagination or are used fictitiously, and any resemblance to actual persons, living or dead, business establishments, events, or locales is entirely coincidental.

DEDICATION

To the One who is always here in spirit we miss you

For the one who walks with me unseen,
In the quiet spaces, your presence keen.
Your voice, a whisper in the wind,
Guiding me where dreams begin.
Though parted by the veil of time,
Your light still shines, a beacon fine.
In each endeavor, every stride,
Your spirit journeys by my side.
This book is born of love and grace,
A tribute to your enduring place.
In every word, your essence flows,
A testament to the bond we chose.

Chapter 1

The autumn breeze rustled through the trees lining Oakbrook's main street, scattering golden leaves across the sidewalk. Sarah Thompson hurried along; her arms full of craft supplies for her third-grade class. The quaint storefronts and historic buildings of downtown Oakbrook provided a picturesque backdrop, but Sarah barely noticed, her mind preoccupied with the day ahead.

As she passed The Cozy Corner Café, the aroma of freshly brewed coffee and cinnamon rolls wafted out, tempting her. Sarah glanced at her watch and sighed. No time for indulgences this morning. She made a mental note to stop by after school; maybe the familiar comfort of her favorite haunt would help clear her mind.

Approaching Oakbrook Elementary, Sarah took a deep breath, steeling herself for another day of challenges and rewards. She loved her students, but lately, a nagging sense of unfulfillment had been creeping into her heart. Was teaching enough? Was she truly making a difference?

"Good morning, Ms. Thompson!" a chirpy voice said. Lucy Davis, a shy eight-year-old with untamed curls, stood at the school entrance, her bright smile contrasting with her worn clothes and scuffed shoes.

Sarah's heart melted. "Good morning, Lucy! Ready for our art project today?"

Lucy nodded enthusiastically, falling into step beside Sarah as they entered the building. "I've been thinking about it all weekend," she

                    SANDRA E SINCLAIR

confided. "Do you think...do you think I could make something for my mom? She's been really sad lately."

Sarah's chest tightened. She knew Lucy's mother struggled to make ends meet after losing her job. "Of course, sweetie. I think that's a wonderful idea. I'm sure it will cheer her up."

As they walked to the classroom, Sarah's colleague and best friend, Emma Rodriguez, stepped beside them. "You're here early," Emma remarked, her dark eyes twinkling with mischief. "Eager to start another day of shaping young minds?"

Sarah laughed, the sound echoing in the empty hallway. "Always. Though I wouldn't mind if God shaped my own a bit more clearly sometimes."

Emma's expression softened. "Still feeling that restlessness, *huh*? Have you prayed about it?"

"Every night," Sarah admitted, lowering her voice as they approached her classroom. "I just feel like there's something more I should be doing, you know? Like God's calling me to stretch beyond these walls."

Emma squeezed her arm. "He'll make it clear in His time, Sarah. You're already doing such important work here."

Sarah nodded, grateful for her friend's encouragement. As Lucy scampered off to her desk, Sarah turned to Emma. "Speaking of stretching, there's a community outreach event next Saturday. Are you going?"

"Wouldn't miss it if you're going." Emma grinned. "Someone's got to keep you from working yourself to the bone. Besides, I hear the new youth pastor at Oakbrook Community Church is quite the charmer." Emma pumped her eyebrows.

Sarah rolled her eyes good-naturedly. "Emma, you know I'm not looking for—"

"I know, I know," Emma interrupted, backing toward the door. "But a little divine intervention never hurt anyone. See you at lunch!"

As her students began to file in, Sarah pushed thoughts of restlessness and divine intervention aside. She had young minds to nurture, and for now, that was enough.

The morning passed in a blur of math lessons and reading circles. As the children worked on their art projects, Sarah moved around the room, offering encouragement and guidance. She paused at Lucy's desk, where the girl was carefully coloring a bright yellow sun.

"That's beautiful, Lucy," Sarah said. "Your mom will love it."

Lucy looked up, her eyes shining. "Do you think...do you think God cares about stuff like this? About making my mom happy?"

Sarah knelt beside the desk, her heart swelling with emotion. "I absolutely do, Lucy. God cares about every part of our lives, especially the love we show to others."

As she stood, Sarah noticed Jayden, a boisterous boy, sitting in the corner. His paper was blank, his crayon untouched. Sarah made her way over, crouching beside him.

"Everything okay, Jayden?" she asked.

Jayden shrugged, not meeting her eyes. "I don't know what to draw," he mumbled.

Sarah studied him for a moment. Jayden had been withdrawn lately, and his usual energy dimmed. "Well," she said, keeping her tone light, "why don't you draw something that makes you happy? Or something you wish for?"

Jayden considered this, then picked up his crayon. As Sarah watched, he began to sketch a rough outline of what looked like a house.

The rest of the day passed in a whirlwind of activity. As the final bell rang and her students filed out, Sarah slumped into her chair, exhausted but contented. She loved these kids, loved watching them learn and grow. But that persistent feeling of something missing nagged at her.

Gathering her things, Sarah decided to take a detour on her way home. The walk to Riverside Park was short, the late afternoon sun casting long shadows across the path. She found a quiet bench overlooking the river and pulled out her Bible.

"Lord," she prayed, "I know You've called me to teach and love these children. But I can't shake this feeling that there's more. More things I could be doing and more ways I could be serving You. Please, show me Your path."

As the sun dipped lower, painting the sky in brilliant oranges and pinks, Sarah felt a sense of peace settle over her. Whatever God had in store, she would trust His timing.

The sun had long since set, but Michael Carter's office light still burned brightly in the otherwise darkened church. He stood at the window, gazing out at the quiet streets of Oakbrook, his reflection a ghostly overlay on the glass. In his hand, he clutched a crumpled letter—his resignation from his previous youth pastor position in his old town.

"Lord," he whispered, "am I really ready for this?"

The doubt gnawing at him since he'd arrived in Oakbrook three weeks ago surged to the forefront of his mind. He turned to his desk, his gaze falling on the neatly organized piles of youth group plans and community outreach ideas. Everything looked perfect on paper, but Michael instinctively felt something was missing.

He picked up a framed photo of his former youth group, smiling faces frozen in joy. They had come so far together and overcome so many challenges. How could he hope to replicate that success here, in this small town where he was a stranger?

Michael's thoughts were interrupted by a soft knock at the door. Pastor David poked his head in, eyebrows rising at the sight of Michael still at work.

"Burning the midnight oil, I see," the older man said, stepping into the office. "Everything alright, son?"

Michael forced a smile. "Just finalizing some plans for the community outreach event this weekend."

Pastor David Peterson nodded, his expression knowing. "And how are you settling in? Really."

The gentle inquiry broke through Michael's constructed facade. He sank into his chair, running a hand through his hair. "I don't know, Pastor. I thought I was ready for this, but now... I'm not so sure. What if I can't connect with these kids? What if I'm not what this church needs?"

The pastor listened and then moved to sit across from Michael. "You know," he said, his voice thoughtful, "when I first came to Oakbrook, I had those same doubts. But I've learned that God doesn't call the equipped. He equips the called."

Michael nodded, the familiar verse bringing a small measure of comfort. "I know that in my head, but my heart...it's having a hard time catching up."

Pastor David leaned forward, his eyes kind but firm. "That's where faith comes in, Michael. Trust that God brought you here for a reason. The connections and the impact will come in time. For now, just be present. Be open to where He leads you."

As the pastor left, Michael turned to his Bible, finding solace in the worn pages. His gaze fell on a passage from Isaiah. "So do not fear, for I am with you; do not be dismayed, for I am your God. I will strengthen and help you; I will uphold you with my righteous right hand."

The words seemed to leap off the page, speaking directly to his doubts. Michael closed his eyes, offering up a prayer. "Lord, I trust in Your plan. Help me to be the leader these kids need, to make a real difference in their lives."

He turned back to his plans for the outreach event. As he worked, an idea began to form—a mentorship program pairing older teens with younger kids in the community. It wasn't much, but it felt like a start, a way to begin building those crucial connections. It was something to think about and flesh out later.

As Michael locked up the church and headed home, he felt a glimmer of hope. Tomorrow would bring its own issues, but for tonight, he had faith that he was where God wanted him to be.

Chapter 2

Across town, Michael stood in front of the floor-length mirror in his small apartment, adjusting his collar for the third time. The crisp, white shirt and dark jeans were a far cry from his usual casual attire, but today wasn't just any day. It was his first official Sunday as the new youth pastor at Oakbrook Community Church.

"Lord," he prayed, "use me today. Help me connect with these kids and show them Your love."

As he grabbed his well-worn Bible from the nightstand, his gaze fell on the faded photograph tucked inside. A younger version of himself stared back, arms slung around two other teenagers, all three sporting cocky grins and questionable fashion choices. A lifetime ago, it seemed.

His heart clenched. How different his life could have been without God's intervention. He traced the faces of his old friends, wondering where they were now. Had they found the peace and purpose he had? Or were they still lost, still searching?

He tucked the photo back into his Bible, a reminder of where he'd come from and the transformative power of faith. "Thank You, God," he whispered, "for never giving up on me."

The drive to the church was short. The streets of Oakbrook were quiet in the early morning light. As Michael pulled into the parking lot, he spotted Pastor David unloading boxes from his car.

"Need a hand?" Michael said, jogging over.

Pastor David's face broke into a warm smile. "Michael! You're right on time. These are for the youth room—I thought we could spruce it up a bit before the kids arrive."

As they carried the boxes inside, Pastor David's expression grew serious. "How are you feeling about today? First impressions are important, but remember, it's not about being cool or popular. It's about..."

"Showing them Christ's love," Michael finished. "I know, Pastor. And honestly? I'm nervous as hell...I mean, heck," he corrected, heat rushing to his cheeks.

Pastor David chuckled. "God can work with nervous. He's had plenty of practice with me over the years. Just be yourself, Michael. That's who He called to this position."

Michael's nerves began to settle as they set up the youth room, hanging posters and arranging chairs. This space, with its worn couches and ping-pong table, felt like home. He could already imagine it filled with teenagers laughing, talking, and seeking answers to life's big questions.

"Oh, before I forget," Pastor David said, pulling something from his pocket, "here's the flyer we're participating in for the community outreach event next Saturday. It would be great if you could get some of the youth group involved."

Michael took the flyer and scanned it. "Absolutely. It's a great opportunity to serve. I've been thinking of some ideas, and I'll mention it to the kids today."

The morning passed in a blur of introductions, worship, and trying to remember dozens of new names. By the time Michael stood in front of the youth group, his nerves had settled into a quiet determination.

"So," he began, looking out at the sea of curious teenage faces, "I know you're all wondering who this new guy is and whether he's going to be as lame as you're afraid he might be."

A ripple of laughter went through the room, and Michael grinned. "Well, I'll let you in on a secret. I used to sit where you're sitting, thinking the exact same thing. And I was pretty sure no one up here could understand what I was going through."

He paused, letting his gaze sweep the room. In the back, a boy with spiky hair and a sullen expression caught his attention. The boy looked away, but not before Michael recognized the defiance and pain in his eyes.

"I was wrong," Michael continued. "Because the truth is, we're all on a journey. And no matter where you are on that journey—whether you've been in church your whole life or this is your first time here, if you're feeling on top of the world or like the world's on top of you—God sees you. He knows you. And He loves you more than you can imagine."

As he launched into the lesson, he felt a familiar warmth in his chest. This was where he wanted to be. These kids, with all their energy, questions, and doubts, were his mission field.

He spoke about identity, about finding their worth in Christ rather than in the world's ever-changing standards. As he talked, he noticed the sullen boy in the back straightening up, his eyes fixed on Michael with an almost unnerving intensity.

"Now," Michael said, wrapping up the lesson, "I've got a challenge for you all. Next Saturday, our church is participating in a community outreach event. It's a chance for us to put our faith into action, to be the hands and feet of Jesus in our community. Who's interested in joining me?"

A few hands went up. Michael smiled, encouraging them. "No pressure. But I promise that serving others is one of the best ways to grow your faith. Plus, it'll be fun. We'll grab lunch afterward, my treat."

After the service, as Michael was gathering his notes, he felt a presence beside him. Looking up, he saw the sullen boy from the back row.

"Hey," Michael said casually. "I'm Michael. What's your name?"

"Tyler," the boy muttered, scuffing his shoe against the carpet. "That stuff you said...about God loving us no matter what. You really believe that?"

Michael's heart went out to the boy. "With every fiber of my being, Tyler. Want to grab a soda and talk about it?"

Tyler hesitated, then nodded. As they walked toward the small kitchen, Michael said a silent prayer of thanks. Reaching out to kids like Tyler was why he'd answered God's call to ministry.

Over sodas and leftover doughnuts from the morning service, Tyler began to open up. He was a sophomore at Oakbrook High, struggling to fit in and feeling pressure from all sides—parents, teachers, and peers.

"I just... I don't know where I belong," Tyler admitted, staring into his soda can. "Everything's changing so fast, and I can't keep up. And God? I don't know. Sometimes it feels like He's a million miles away."

Michael nodded, remembering his own tumultuous teenage years. "I get it, Tyler. I really do. But here's the thing—God isn't far away. He's right here, right now. Sometimes, we just need to quiet all the noise around us to hear Him."

Tyler looked up, a glimmer of hope in his eyes. "How do I do that?"

Michael smiled. "Well, that's something we can work on together. Why don't you come to the outreach event next Saturday? It might help to get out of your own head for a bit and focus on helping others."

Tyler agreed, and as he left, Michael felt a surge of purpose. This was just the beginning, he knew. There were so many kids like Tyler out there, searching for meaning, for belonging. And maybe God had placed Michael here to help them find it.

As he locked up the church, his mind drifted to the outreach event. He wondered what kind of impact they might make; what lives might be touched.

———— ❧ ————

The last rays of sunlight filtered through the empty sanctuary's stained glass windows as Michael slumped into a pew. His first official Sunday had been a storm of emotions, and now, in the quiet aftermath, he felt the weight of responsibility settling on his shoulders.

He pulled out his phone, thumbing through the list of names and notes he'd made about the teens he'd met. There were so many stories, so many struggles. Tyler's face flashed in his mind, the boy's words echoing in his ears, "Sometimes it feels like He's a million miles away."

"Lord," Michael whispered, his voice barely audible in the cavernous space, "how do I bridge that gap?"

As if in answer, his phone buzzed with a text from Pastor David. "Great job today. Remember, Rome wasn't built in a day. Take it one step at a time."

Michael smiled wryly. One step at a time. But what if he took a misstep? What if he let these kids down?

Unable to shake his restlessness, Michael found himself in the youth room, surveying the space with fresh eyes. The worn couches and faded posters seemed inadequate. How could he create an environment where kids like Tyler felt welcome and seen?

He smiled as he got an idea. What if they redesigned the space together? Let the teens take ownership and express their faith and personalities through art, music, or whatever spoke to them.

Energized by the concept, he began sketching out a plan. He was so engrossed that he didn't hear the approaching footsteps until a voice startled him.

"Burning the midnight oil already?"

Michael looked up to see Mrs. Henderson, the elderly church secretary, standing in the doorway.

"Just coming up with some ideas," he explained, gesturing to his notes.

Mrs. Henderson smiled. "You remind me of our last youth pastor when he first started. Full of energy and big dreams." Her expression softened. "He burned out after a year. Tried to do too much, too fast."

Michael felt a flicker of unease. "I appreciate the concern, Mrs. Henderson, but I really feel called to make some changes here."

The older woman nodded. "Change can be good, dear. But remember, this church has a history. These kids have a history. Don't be so eager to make your mark that you forget to honor what came before."

As Mrs. Henderson bid him good night, Michael grappled with a new issue. How could he bring fresh energy and ideas to the youth ministry without alienating the existing church community?

Seeking guidance, he opened his Bible, finding comfort in the familiar words of Ecclesiastes. "There is a time for everything and a season for every activity under the heavens."

Michael closed his eyes, praying, "Lord, grant me wisdom. Help me discern the right time for change and the patience to build trust. Show me how to honor the past while embracing the future You have for this ministry."

Michael felt excitement and trepidation as he locked up the church and headed home. The road ahead wouldn't be easy, but he was beginning to see that the challenges—bridging the gap between the teens and their faith, balancing new ideas with established traditions—were all part of God's plan for growth.

In his apartment, he pinned his sketches for the youth room redesign on the wall alongside the flyer for the upcoming outreach event. Two first steps on a journey he was only beginning to understand.

Before turning in, he sent a quick text to Tyler. *Glad you're coming Saturday. Looking forward to serving together.*

As he drifted to sleep, Michael's dreams were filled with images of transformed lives and a thriving youth ministry.

Sarah Thompson stared at the flyer for the community outreach event, her fingers tracing the bold letters announcing, "Oakbrook Community Church Youth Group." The paper trembled in her hand, a physical manifestation of the restlessness growing in her heart.

"Is this what You're calling me to, Lord?" she whispered, her voice a quiet note in the empty classroom.

The last bell had rung hours ago, but Sarah lingered, unable to shake the feeling that something was about to change. Her gaze drifted to the colorful artwork adorning the walls, evidence of her students' creativity and growth. She loved teaching, but the nagging sense of unfulfillment kept creeping into her heart.

A knock on the door startled her from her reverie. Emma poked her head in. "Still here? Don't tell me you're planning more lessons on a Friday night."

Sarah managed a smile, tucking the flyer into her desk drawer. "Just lost in thought, I guess."

Emma's eyes narrowed, concern evident in her expression. "Sarah, talk to me. What's going on?"

Taking a deep breath, Sarah confessed the doubts plaguing her. "I love teaching, Emma. I do. But lately, I feel that there's...more. That God's calling me to something else, something bigger."

As she shared her heart, Sarah felt relief and apprehension. Saying it out loud made it real and terrifying.

Emma listened, her expression thoughtful. "Have you considered volunteering somewhere? Maybe exploring different ministries in the community?"

Sarah's heart skipped a beat, thinking of the flyer hidden in her desk. "I've thought about it," she admitted. "But, Emma, what if it interferes with my teaching? What if I'm not cut out for anything else?"

Emma reached out, squeezing Sarah's hand. "Sarah, I've seen you with these kids. You have a gift for connecting with them, for seeing their potential. Maybe God's trying to show you how to use that gift differently. Just don't take on anything too heavy. Your health is important too."

As they talked, Sarah felt excitement kindling in her chest. The idea of expanding her horizons, of finding new ways to serve and make a difference, stirred something deep within her.

"Okay," she said tentatively, flashing Emma a smile. "I'll look into some volunteer opportunities. Just to check things out."

Emma grinned, pulling Sarah into a hug. "That's my girl. Who knows? This could be the start of something amazing."

As Sarah drove home that evening, her mind was a whirlwind of thoughts and possibilities. She raised her voice, a whisper over the engine's hum, "Lord, if this is where you're leading me, please make it clear. And if not...well, help me trust Your plan."

Chapter 3

Sarah's hand hovered over the box of donated books, her heart racing. A small, leather-bound Bible caught her eye among the worn covers and dog-eared pages. Its golden edges glinted in the fluorescent light of the church basement, seeming to beckon her. As she reached for it, another hand brushed against hers.

"Oh, I'm sorry," a deep voice chuckled. "Ladies first."

Sarah looked up, meeting the warm, brown eyes of a man she didn't recognize. His easy smile and the paint-splattered T-shirt suggested he was as comfortable in this cluttered space as much as she felt out of place.

"I'm Michael," he said, extending his hand. "The new youth pastor."

"Sarah," she replied, shaking his hand and hoping her palm wasn't as clammy as it felt. "I teach at Oakbrook Elementary."

Michael's eyes lit up. "A teacher! That's fantastic. We could really use your expertise here. Have you volunteered with the church before?"

Sarah shook her head, feeling self-conscious. "No, this is my first time. I just felt...called, I guess. To do something more."

Michael nodded, understanding in his eyes. "That calling can be pretty powerful, can't it? Well, Sarah, welcome to the chaos. We're sorting donations for the community outreach event next weekend. Think you can handle it?"

Sarah laughed, some of her nervousness melting away. "I wrangle third-graders every day. This should be a piece of cake."

As they worked side by side, sorting books and chatting, Sarah found herself relaxing. Michael was easy to talk to, and his passion for his work was evident in every word. She learned that he'd only been in Oakbrook for a few weeks, that he loved basketball, and hated coffee, ("I know, it's sacrilegious in this town," he joked), and that he had a particular soft heart for troubled teens.

"There's this one kid, Tyler," Michael was saying, his brow furrowed in concern. "He's got so much potential, but he's struggling. I'm trying to get him more involved, but it's like pulling teeth."

Sarah nodded. "I have a few students like that. Sometimes all it takes is one person believing in them to make a difference."

"Exactly!" Michael exclaimed, his eyes lighting up. "That's why I became a youth pastor. To be that person for kids who might not have anyone else."

As the afternoon wore on, Sarah shared more about her own journey—her love for teaching, her growing sense that God was calling her to do more, and her uncertainty about what that "more" might be.

"Have you ever considered getting involved in youth ministry?" Michael asked, his tone casual but his eyes keen.

Sarah blinked, surprised. "Me? Oh, I don't know. I love working with younger kids, but teenagers...they're a whole different ballgame."

Michael laughed. "They're not as scary as they seem, I promise. Look, we're always looking for volunteers for our after-school program. Why don't you come by sometime and see if it's something you might be interested in?"

Sarah hesitated. The idea was both exciting and terrifying. Could this be the "more" she'd been searching for?

"I'll think about it," she said.

As they continued sorting through the donations, Sarah's mind wandered to her classroom. She thought of Lucy, the shy girl with the bright smile, and Jayden, the usually boisterous boy who had been so quiet lately. She wondered if the struggles these children faced were similar to those of the teenagers Michael worked with.

"You know," Sarah said, breaking a moment of comfortable silence, "I've been noticing some changes in my students lately. It's not just about teaching them math and reading anymore. Some of them are dealing with really tough situations at home."

Michael nodded, his expression serious. "It's hard, isn't it? Seeing them struggle and feeling like there's only so much you can do."

"Exactly." Sarah sighed. "I try to be there for them, to create a safe space in my classroom, but sometimes it feels like it's not enough."

Michael put down the book he was holding and turned to face her. "Sarah, what you're doing is incredibly important. You're planting seeds of hope and love in those kids' lives. Sometimes, we don't get to see the fruit of our labor right away, but trust me, it makes a difference."

His words warmed her heart, and she felt a sudden surge of gratitude for this unexpected encounter. Here was someone who understood the dynamics and the joys of working with young people, someone who shared her desire to make a real difference in their lives.

As they finished up for the day, Sarah felt excitement at the prospect of new opportunities, nervousness about stepping out of her comfort zone, and an unexpected flutter whenever Michael smiled at her.

"Thanks for your help today, Sarah," Michael said as they walked out to the parking lot. "Will I see you at the outreach event next weekend?"

She nodded, surprised to realize how much she was looking forward to it. "I wouldn't miss it."

As she drove home, her mind was buzzing with possibilities. The afternoon had been more than just sorting books—it felt like the first step on a new path. But where would that path lead?

She said a silent prayer. "Lord, if this is where You're leading me, please make it clear. And if not...well, help me to trust Your plan."

That evening, as Sarah prepared for bed, she reached for her Bible. She opened it to the book of Proverbs, with a familiar verse. "Trust in the Lord with all your heart and lean not on your own understanding; in all your ways submit to him, and he will make your paths straight" (Proverbs 3:5-6).

The words seemed to leap off the page, speaking directly to her heart. Sarah closed her eyes, letting the verse wash over her. "Okay, Lord," she whispered. "I'm trusting You. Whatever You have in store, I'm ready."

With a sense of peace settling over her, she drifted off to sleep. Her dreams were filled with images of smiling children, stacks of books, and warm, brown eyes that seemed to see right into her soul.

The church was quiet as Michael locked up, the echo of the key turning in the lock reverberating through the empty halls. He paused at the top of the basement stairs; his gaze drawn to the box of sorted books—a tangible reminder of the afternoon's unexpected encounter.

Sarah's words about her students lingered in his mind, stirring a mix of emotions he couldn't quite name. He grappled with a familiar sense of inadequacy as he made his way to his office. How could he hope to make a real difference in these kids' lives when there was so much he didn't understand about their struggles?

Slumping into his chair, his gaze fell on the youth group attendance sheet from last Sunday. Tyler's name jumped out at him, and the blank space beside it was a stark reminder of the teen's absence. He'd promised to attend the outreach event, but Michael instinctively felt he was losing his tenuous connection with the troubled boy.

"Lord," he whispered, running a hand through his hair, "am I in over my head here?"

As if in answer, his phone buzzed with a text from Pastor David. *How did the sorting go? Any potential volunteers for the youth program?*

Michael's thoughts went to Sarah. Her passion for her students, her desire to do more—it all resonated with him. But as he began to type a response, doubt crept in. Was he letting his personal feelings cloud his judgment? Was he too eager to bring her into the youth ministry simply because he enjoyed her company?

Seeking guidance, he reached for his Bible, letting it fall open. His eyes landed on a passage from 1 Corinthians. "God has arranged the parts in the body, every one of them, just as he wanted them to be."

The words sparked a thought. What if the youth ministry wasn't meant to be his sole responsibility? What if God was bringing people like Sarah into his life to create a more holistic approach to supporting these kids?

Energized by this new perspective, he texted Pastor David back, then began sketching out a plan for a mentorship program, connecting volunteers from different areas of expertise with the teens who needed them most. He could envision how Sarah's experience with younger kids could benefit someone like Tyler, bridging the gap between childhood and adolescence.

As the plan took shape, Michael felt inspired to act. This wasn't just about him anymore—it was about creating a network of support, a community that could make a difference in these young lives.

Before heading home, Michael sent a quick text to Tyler. *I missed you on Sunday. I hope everything's okay. I'm looking forward to seeing you at the outreach event.*

As he drove through the quiet streets of Oakbrook, Michael's mind was racing with possibilities. The afternoon with Sarah opened his eyes to new ways of approaching his ministry and new avenues for reaching these kids. But with that excitement came a nagging worry—was he ready for the changes this might bring, both professionally and personally?

Pulling into his driveway, he offered up a prayer, "Lord, guide my steps. Help me to be open to Your plan, even if it looks different than what I imagined. And if Sarah is meant to be part of this ministry, show me how to navigate that with wisdom and integrity."

That night, as he drifted to sleep, his dreams were a mix of smiling teens eagerly learning and involved, and a pair of kind eyes that seemed to understand the weight of their calling.

Chapter 4

The shrill ring of the school bell cut through the chaos of the playground, signaling the end of recess. As Sarah herded her class back inside, she noticed Lucy hanging back, her usual bounce missing from her step.

"Lucy?" Sarah called. "Is everything okay?"

The little girl looked up, her eyes brimming with unshed tears. "Ms. Thompson, can I talk to you? In private?"

Sarah's heart clenched. "Of course, sweetie. Let's settle everyone, and then you and I can chat."

As the other students filed into the classroom, chattering about their playground adventures, Sarah's mind raced. What could be troubling Lucy? The girl had seemed fine earlier in the day, showing off the picture she'd drawn for her mother.

Once the class was engrossed in their reading assignment, Sarah beckoned Lucy to her desk.

"What's on your mind, Lucy?" she asked.

Lucy twisted the hem of her shirt, her eyes fixed on the floor. "Ms. Thompson, is it bad to pray for something you really, really want?"

Sarah blinked, surprised by the question. "Of course not, Lucy. God wants us to bring all our desires to Him. Why do you ask?"

"Because..." Lucy's voice hitched. "Because I've been praying really hard for my mom to get a job, but it's not happening. And now...now we might have to move away."

Sarah's heart sank. She'd known Lucy's family was struggling, but she hadn't realized things had gotten so dire.

"Oh, Lucy," she said, reaching out to squeeze the girl's hand. "I'm so sorry you're going through this. But I want you to know something very important. God always hears our prayers, even when it doesn't seem like it."

Lucy looked up, her eyes shining with hope and doubt. "But if He hears them, why doesn't He answer?"

Sarah took a deep breath, praying for wisdom. How could she explain the complexities of faith to an eight-year-old?

"Sometimes," she began, "God answers our prayers in ways we don't expect. And sometimes, He has a bigger plan that we can't see yet. But no matter what, He loves you and your mom very much, and He's always with you."

As she spoke, an idea popped into Sarah's mind. The community outreach event at the church—hadn't Michael mentioned a job fair?

"Lucy," she said, her excitement growing, "I think I might have an idea that could help. But I need to make a phone call first. Can you be my special helper and make sure everyone's reading quietly while I step out for a minute?"

Lucy nodded, a small smile breaking through her tears.

In the hallway, Sarah pulled out her phone, her fingers shaking as she dialed the number Michael had given her.

"Hello?" His warm voice answered on the second ring.

"Michael? It's Sarah. From the book sorting yesterday? I'm sorry to bother you, but I have a question about the outreach event..."

As Sarah explained Lucy's situation, she could hear the excitement growing in Michael's voice.

"Sarah, this is perfect," he said. "We're actually partnering with several local businesses for the job fair portion of the event. I can't make any promises, but I'd be happy to pass along Lucy's mom's information to some of our contacts."

Relief washed over Sarah. "That would be wonderful, Michael. Thank you so much."

"No need to thank me," he replied. She could hear the smile in his voice. "This is what the event is for—bringing the community together to help each other. Oh, and, Sarah? I meant what I said yesterday. We could really use someone like you in our youth program. Just...think about it, okay?"

As she hung up, she felt a renewed sense of purpose. This was what it meant to put faith into action—to be Jesus's hands and feet in her community.

Back in the classroom, she knelt at her desk beside Lucy. "I have some good news," she whispered. "There's going to be a special event at my church this weekend, with lots of fun activities for kids and a job fair for grown-ups. Do you think your mom might like to come?"

Lucy's face lit up. "Really? Oh, Ms. Thompson, thank you!"

As Sarah watched Lucy practically skip back to her seat, she offered a silent prayer of thanks. She didn't know what would come of this—whether Lucy's mom would find a job or whether their situation would improve—but she knew that in this moment, she had been able to offer hope. And sometimes, that was enough.

The rest of the school day passed in a blur, Sarah's mind continually drifting to the upcoming outreach event. As she was packing up to leave, a knock on her classroom door startled her.

"Come in," she called, expecting to see a fellow teacher or perhaps a parent.

Instead, Michael's familiar face appeared around the door. "I hope I'm not interrupting," he said with a grin. "I was in the neighborhood and thought I'd drop off some flyers for the outreach event. I figured you might want to hand them out to your students' families."

Sarah blinked, surprised but pleased. "That's so thoughtful, thank you. I was just thinking about the event."

As Michael stepped into the classroom, Sarah noticed how at ease he seemed, even in this unfamiliar environment. He moved around the room, taking in the colorful artwork on the walls and the neatly arranged desks.

"This is a great space," he said in genuine admiration. "You can really feel the love and care you put into it."

Sarah felt a warmth spread through her as she heard his words. "Thank you. It's not always easy, but these kids...they're worth every minute."

Michael nodded, his expression serious. "I can see that. You know, Sarah, that's the kind of passion we need in our youth program. Have you given any more thought to volunteering?"

She hesitated. The idea was still daunting, but after her conversation with Lucy, something had shifted. She felt a pull, a sense that God was opening a door.

"I have," she said. "And I think... I think I'd like to give it a try."

Michael's face broke into a wide grin. "That's fantastic! I promise you won't regret it. These kids have so much potential. Sometimes, they just need someone to believe in them."

As they chatted about the details of the youth program and the upcoming event, Sarah felt a growing sense of excitement. This felt right, like a piece of a puzzle falling into place.

When Michael left, promising to see her at the outreach event, Sarah sat at her desk for a long moment, lost in thought. She pulled out her Bible, flipping to a familiar passage in Jeremiah.

"For I know the plans I have for you," declares the Lord, "plans to prosper you and not to harm you, plans to give you hope and a future."

Sarah traced the words with her finger, a smile playing on her lips. She didn't know what God had in store for her, but for the first time in a long time, she felt like she was on the right path.

As she gathered her things to leave, her phone buzzed with a text from Emma. *Saw the new youth pastor leaving your classroom. Spill the tea, girl!* And she'd sent a winking emoji face.

Sarah laughed, shaking her head. She typed out a quick reply. *Nothing to spill. Just talking about the outreach event. And...I might be volunteering with the youth program.*

Emma's response was immediate. *What?! Okay, we need wine and a full debrief. My place, 7 o'clock. No excuses!*

Driving home, her mind was in overdrive. The issues facing Lucy and her family, the excitement of new opportunities with the youth program, and yes, the unexpected flutter she felt when she thought of Michael's smile.

"Lord," she prayed, "I don't know where all this is leading, but I trust You. Help me to be open to Your plan, whatever it may be."

As Michael left the elementary school, the setting sun painted Oakbrook's streets in hues of orange and purple. His mind buzzed with the unexpected encounter with Sarah, her agreement to volunteer, and the palpable excitement he'd felt in her classroom. As he drove, a nagging thought wormed its way into his consciousness. Was he letting his growing attraction to Sarah cloud his judgment about her involvement in the youth program?

At a red light, his gaze fell on the stack of outreach event flyers on the passenger seat. The job fair portion stood out, Sarah's concern for Lucy and her mother echoing in his mind. A sudden realization hit him. How many other families in their community were struggling in silence, their needs unknown to the church?

Pulling into the church parking lot, he was surprised to see Pastor David's car still there. He found the older man in his office, poring over the church budget.

"Michael," Pastor David greeted him, his brow furrowed. "Good timing. We might have a problem with the outreach event."

Michael's heart sank as Pastor David explained. The main sponsor for the job fair had pulled out, leaving them scrambling to fill the gap. "Without those connections, I'm not sure how effective our job fair will be," Pastor David concluded.

The weight of responsibility settled on Michael's shoulders. He thought of Lucy's mother, of all the people counting on this event for a chance at a better life.

"We can't cancel it," he said firmly. "There has to be another way."

As they brainstormed solutions, Michael drew on unexpected resources. He mentioned Sarah's connection to the school and the potential to reach more families in need.

An idea came to him—what if they expanded their outreach beyond the church walls, partnering with local schools and community centers?

Pastor David listened, his expression thoughtful. "That's thinking outside the box, Michael. But it's a lot to take on. Are you sure you're ready for that kind of responsibility?"

Michael hesitated. The task seemed daunting, but he couldn't ignore the image of hope on Sarah's face when he'd offered to help Lucy's family. "I have to try," he said. "Isn't this why God called me here? To make a real difference in this community?"

As they fleshed out the new plan, Michael felt some trepidation but also excitement. This was bigger than anything he'd taken on before, and success was far from guaranteed. But with each step, he felt a growing certainty that this was the right path.

Later that night, as Michael prepared for bed, his phone buzzed with a text from Sarah. *Thank you again for today. It means so much to Lucy and her mom to have this opportunity.*

Michael smiled, warmth spreading through him. *Happy to help. I look forward to working with you on this and future projects.*

As he set his phone down, he caught sight of his reflection in the mirror. The man looking back at him seemed different somehow—more purposeful, more grounded. He realized that in reaching out to help others, he was finding a deeper sense of his own calling.

Kneeling by his bed, he offered a prayer. "Lord, guide me in this new endeavor. Help me to be a vessel for Your love in this community. And...if it's Your will, show me how Sarah fits into your plan for me."

As he drifted to sleep, Michael's dreams were filled with images of a thriving community, lives transformed by God's love. And through it all, a pair of kind eyes and a warm smile that made his heart race in a way he hadn't felt in years.

Chapter 5

The community center buzzed with activity, a sea of colorful booths, and eager faces. Sarah stood at the entrance, a bundle of nerves and excitement. She clutched a stack of flyers for the tutoring program, her lifeline in this unfamiliar territory. As she scanned the crowd, her eyes landed on a familiar face—Michael, surrounded by a group of teenagers, his laugh carrying across the room.

Their eyes met, and Michael's face lit up with a smile that made Sarah's heart skip. He waved her over, and as she made her way through the crowd, she had a feeling that this day would change her life.

"Sarah! You made it," Michael greeted her. "Everyone, this is Ms. Thompson. She's going to be helping out with our youth program."

The teenagers regarded her with curiosity and skepticism. One girl with vibrant blue hair and multiple piercings raised an eyebrow. "You're a teacher, right? Are you going to make us do homework?"

Sarah laughed, feeling some of her tension ease. "Only if you want to. I'm here to help, not to assign pop quizzes."

As the teens chuckled, Sarah noticed one boy hanging back, his eyes downcast. She recognized him from Michael's description—Tyler, the troubled teen he'd mentioned. Sarah made a mental note to try to connect with him later.

Before she could say anything, a commotion near the job fair section caught everyone's attention. Sarah's heart leaped when she saw Lucy and her mother looking lost and overwhelmed amidst the bustle.

"Excuse me," Sarah said to the group, her teacher instincts kicking in. "I need to help someone."

As she approached them, Sarah said a silent prayer, "Lord, guide my words. Help me be a light in their darkness."

"Mrs. Davis?" Sarah said. "I'm Sarah Thompson, Lucy's teacher. I'm so glad you could make it."

Relief washed over Mrs. Davis's face. "Ms. Thompson! Lucy's been talking about you non-stop. Thank you for telling us about this event."

Sarah smiled, crouching down to Lucy's level. "And how are you doing, Lucy? Are you excited to be here?"

Lucy nodded; her eyes wide as she took in the bustling event.

"Why don't I show you around?" Sarah offered, standing up. "I heard there's a great booth for job seekers just over there."

As they made their way through the crowd, Sarah noticed Michael watching her, a look of admiration on his face. She felt a warmth spread through her, a mixture of pride in her ability to help and something else she wasn't quite ready to name.

Sarah guided Mrs. Davis to the job fair section, introducing her to a few employers she had met earlier. As they chatted, Sarah noticed Lucy fidgeting.

"Hey, Lucy," Sarah said, "I saw a face painting booth by the entrance. Would you like to check it out while your mom talks to these nice people?"

Lucy's face lit up, and Mrs. Davis looked gratefully at Sarah. As they walked to the booth, Lucy slipped her small hand into Sarah's, the gesture of trust warming her heart.

"Ms. Thompson," Lucy said, "I know you said that God listens to kids' prayers too. Are you sure about that?"

Sarah's breath caught at the unexpected question. She knelt down to Lucy's level, meeting her earnest gaze. "Of course He does, sweetie. God loves to hear from all His children, no matter how old or young they are. What made you say that?"

Lucy bit her lip, her eyes welling with tears. "I remembered what you said, and I've been praying real hard for my mom to find a job. But it hasn't happened yet." She sighed and shook her head. "Maybe I'm not doing it right!"

Sarah's heart ached for the little girl. She pulled Lucy into a gentle hug, stroking her hair. "Oh, Lucy. You're doing it perfectly. Sometimes, God doesn't answer our prayers right away or in the way we expect. But He always hears us and cares. We just have to trust His timing."

As Lucy nodded against her shoulder, Sarah felt an overwhelming drive ignite within her. This was why she was here—not just to teach but to nurture, guide, and be a beacon of hope in these children's lives.

The afternoon flew by in a whirlwind of introductions, conversations, and small victories. Sarah moved between helping Mrs. Davis navigate the job fair and assisting Michael with the youth group activities. It was exhausting but exhilarating.

As the event wound down, Sarah found a quiet moment with Michael. "This was amazing," she said, feeling like her eyes were lit up and shining. "I've never seen the community come together like this."

Michael's expression was serious as he nodded. "It's what the church should be—a force for good in the community. But, Sarah, I have to ask...are you sure about volunteering with the youth group? It's not always this exciting. There will be tough days, challenging kids."

She took a deep breath, thinking of Tyler's guarded expression and Lucy's shy smile. "I'm sure," she said. "I feel like this is where God is calling me."

Michael's face broke into a wide grin. "I was hoping you'd say that. Welcome aboard, Sarah."

As they shook hands, she felt a spark of electricity between them. She pulled away; her cheeks flushed. "I should go check on Mrs. Davis," she mumbled, hurrying off.

That night, as she reflected on the day's events, she felt excited but also some trepidation. She'd taken a big step today, committing to something new and challenging. But as she opened her Bible to her daily devotion, her gaze landed on a familiar verse.

"For I know the plans I have for you," declares the Lord, "plans to prosper you and not to harm you, plans to give you hope and a future." (Jeremiah 29:11)

Sarah smiled, feeling a sense of peace settle over her. Whatever lay ahead, she knew she wasn't facing it alone. She began jotting down ideas for the youth group, her mind buzzing with possibilities.

As she wrote, she thought of Michael's warm smile, his faith, and how he seemed to bring out the best in everyone around him. But she pushed the thought aside, focusing on her plans.

The last volunteer had long since left, but Michael lingered in the now-quiet community center, his mind replaying the day's events. The success of the outreach event should have filled him with pure joy, but an unexpected undercurrent of anxiety tugged at his thoughts.

His gaze fell on the job fair booth where he'd watched Sarah guide Lucy's mother through the process. Her natural ability to connect with both children and adults had been impressive, to say the least. But it was the way his heart had raced when their eyes met across the room that gave him pause.

"Lord," he whispered into the empty space, "what am I doing?"

As if in answer, his phone buzzed with a text from Pastor David. *Great job today. We're having a board meeting tomorrow to discuss the next steps. 9 a.m. sharp.*

Michael's stomach clenched. The board meeting. In the excitement of the event, he'd almost forgotten. They would want a full report, including his plans for expanding the youth ministry—plans that now heavily involved Sarah.

He went to the small office he'd been using, pulling out his notes. As he began to outline his report, he struggled to maintain objectivity.

Every mention of Sarah's contributions sent a warm flush through his body. Was he emphasizing her role too much? Not enough?

Frustrated, he leaned back in his chair, looking at a framed quote on the wall. "The heart of man plans his way, but the Lord establishes his steps." (Proverbs 16:9)

The verse hit him like a gentle rebuke. Was he trying too hard to control this situation? To define Sarah's role based on his own emerging feelings?

Taking a deep breath, he closed his eyes and began to pray. "Father, I need Your guidance. Help me to see clearly and to lead wisely. If Sarah's involvement in this ministry is part of Your plan, show me how to navigate this without compromising my integrity or the work You've called me to do."

As he prayed, a sense of calm began to settle over him. He realized that his anxiety stemmed not just from his feelings for Sarah but from a deeper fear of failing in his calling. Opening his eyes, he turned back to his notes with renewed focus.

He began to revise his report, emphasizing the community's response to the outreach event, the connections made, and the lives potentially changed. Sarah's contributions were noted as part of a larger picture of community involvement and volunteer engagement.

As he worked, an old idea resurfaced. If they could create a mentorship program, pairing experienced volunteers with the youth group members, it would provide more support for the teens. And it would allow Sarah to be involved without putting undue pressure on their developing relationship.

Energized by this new direction, Michael lost track of time, fleshing out the mentorship program and how it could integrate with their existing activities. When he looked up, the first light of dawn was peeking through the windows.

Gathering his notes, he felt a mix of exhaustion and anticipation. The board meeting would be challenging, but he felt prepared. More than that, he felt aligned with his purpose, his personal feelings taking a backseat to the larger mission of serving the community and guiding these young people.

As he locked up the community center, Michael's phone buzzed with another text. This time, it was from Sarah. *Still processing yesterday. So grateful for the opportunity to be part of this. See you at the next youth group meeting?*

Michael smiled. *Absolutely. Your help was invaluable. I'm looking forward to discussing some new ideas with you.*

Driving home for a quick shower before the board meeting, he felt a sense of peace. Whatever challenges lay ahead—in the youth ministry, in his relationship with Sarah, and in his own spiritual journey—he knew that God was guiding his steps.

Chapter 6

The shrill ring of the school bell jolted Sarah from her reverie. She blinked, realizing she'd been staring at the same math problem for five minutes, her mind wandering to the upcoming youth group meeting.

As her students filed out for recess, Sarah noticed Jayden hanging back, his usual exuberance subdued. "Jayden?" she called. "Is everything okay?"

The boy shrugged, avoiding her gaze. "It's nothing, Ms. Thompson."

Sarah's heart clenched. She'd noticed Jayden's withdrawal over the past week but hadn't found the right moment to address it. Now, with the classroom empty and Jayden's defenses down, she sensed an opportunity.

"You know," she said, "I'm going to be helping out with the youth group at Oakbrook Community Church. They have some pretty cool activities planned. Would you be interested in checking it out?"

Jayden's head snapped up, a mixture of surprise and interest in his eyes. "Really? You're gonna be there?"

Sarah nodded, feeling a glimmer of hope. "Really. And I'd love to see you there."

As Jayden hurried off to join his friends, she sent up a silent prayer of thanks. It wasn't much, but it was a start.

That afternoon, as she gathered her things to head to the youth group meeting, her phone buzzed with a text from Emma.

Good luck with the teen wrangling! Don't forget our wine date tomorrow—I want ALL the details about you and the hot youth pastor. Another winking emoji.

Sarah rolled her eyes but couldn't suppress a smile. *It's not like that! Michael and I are just colleagues. See you tomorrow x.*

As she pulled into the church parking lot, her stomach was a knot of nerves. She spotted Michael unloading boxes from his car and hurried over to help.

"Sarah!" he greeted her with a warm smile. "Ready for your first official youth group meeting?"

Before she could answer, a voice said from across the parking lot. "Ms. Thompson?"

Sarah turned to see Jayden approaching, his mother close behind.

"Jayden! I'm so glad you came," Sarah exclaimed, her face lighting up.

As she made introductions, she noticed how Michael welcomed Jayden and his mother, putting them at ease with his easy charm and genuine warmth.

The youth room was a cacophony of noise and energy as teenagers filtered in. For a moment, Sarah felt overwhelmed, but Michael's steady presence beside her was reassuring.

"Alright, everyone!" Michael said, his voice cutting through the chatter. "We've got a special guest today. This is Ms. Thompson, and she's going to be helping out with our group from now on."

Sarah waved, feeling all eyes on her. "Hi, everyone. I'm excited to be here and get to know all of you."

As the meeting progressed, she was drawn into conversations with the teens. She was surprised by their openness and their willingness to share their struggles and doubts.

During a group discussion about peer pressure, Sarah noticed Tyler—the troubled teen Michael had mentioned—sitting apart from the others, his body language closed off.

Taking a deep breath, she approached him. "Mind if I joined you?"

Tyler shrugged but didn't object. Sarah sat down, letting the silence stretch between them for a moment.

"You know," she finally said, "when I was your age, I thought I had everything figured out. But looking back, I realize how much I was struggling to fit in, to find my place."

Tyler glanced at her, a flicker of interest in his eyes. "Yeah? What changed?"

Sarah smiled. "I found my faith. Or rather, I really embraced it for the first time. It gave me a foundation, a sense of purpose."

Tyler was quiet for a long moment. When he spoke, his voice was barely a whisper. "Sometimes I feel like...like God's given up on me, you know? Like I'm too messed up for Him to care."

Sarah's heart ached at the pain in his voice. "Tyler, look at me," she said. When he met her gaze, she continued, "God will never, ever give up on you. No matter what you've done, no matter how far you think you've strayed, He's always there, waiting with open arms."

As she spoke, she noticed Michael watching them from across the room, a look of approval on his face and felt a surge of confidence.

The rest of the meeting flew by, and before Sarah knew it, they were cleaning up. As she helped stack chairs, Michael approached her.

"You were amazing today," he said, his voice warm with admiration. "The way you connected with Tyler...I've been trying to reach him for a while."

Sarah felt a blush creeping up her neck. "I just spoke from the heart. I remember what it was like to feel lost at that age."

Michael nodded, his expression thoughtful. "That's why we need you here, Sarah. You bring a perspective these kids can relate to."

As they finished cleaning, her mind was buzzing with ideas for future meetings, ways to engage the teens and help them grow in their faith.

"Michael," she said, "I was thinking...what if we started a mentoring program? Pairing some of the older teens with the younger ones?"

His face lit up. "That's a fantastic idea! I'm glad you mentioned it. I've been turning that idea around in my mind for a little while now." He smiled. "It would give the older kids a sense of responsibility, and the younger ones would have someone to look up to."

As they discussed the details, Sarah felt a growing sense of excitement. This was more than just volunteering—it was a chance to make a real difference in these kids' lives.

As they walked to their cars, Michael turned to Sarah. "Listen, I was wondering...would you like to grab coffee sometime? To discuss the mentoring program, of course," he added quickly, heat rushing to his cheeks, his hand clasping the back of his neck.

Sarah felt her heart skip a beat. "I'd like that," she said, hoping her voice sounded steadier than she felt.

That night, as she prepared for bed, she couldn't stop smiling. The day had been difficult but incredibly rewarding. She felt like she was finally stepping into the purpose God had for her.

Opening her Bible for her nightly devotion, the passage stood out. "Therefore, my dear brothers and sisters, stand firm. Let nothing move you. Always give yourselves fully to the work of the Lord, because you know that your labor in the Lord is not in vain." (1 Corinthians 15:58)

As she drifted off, her mind wandered to her upcoming coffee meeting—a date with Michael? Sarah pushed the thought aside. Whatever it was, she was looking forward to it more than she cared to admit.

The clock on Michael's nightstand blinked at 2:37 a.m., but sleep eluded him. His mind raced with thoughts of the youth group meeting, Sarah's natural connection with the teens, and the coffee...meeting.

Date? He'd impulsively suggested. Rolling over, he reached for his Bible, seeking solace in familiar verses.

As he flipped through the pages, the photo he kept in there fluttered out—a reminder of his life before his calling to ministry. Three grinning teenagers, arms slung around each other, eyes bright with mischief and something darker. Michael stared at his younger self, remembering the lost boy he'd been, the choices that had nearly derailed his life.

"Lord," he whispered into the darkness, "am I the right person to guide these kids? To work alongside someone like Sarah?"

The question hung in the air, unanswered. His thoughts drifted to Tyler, the pain in the boy's eyes mirroring his own teenage struggles. And then to Sarah, her gentle approach breaking through Tyler's defenses in a way Michael hadn't been able to.

Sitting up, he reached for his journal. As he began to write, pouring out his doubts and fears, a verse came to mind. "But he said to me, 'My grace is sufficient for you, for my power is made perfect in weakness.'" (2 Corinthians 12:9)

The words resonated. Maybe it was because of his past that he could connect with these teens. And perhaps Sarah's different perspective was what the ministry needed.

He started sketching out ideas for the mentoring program Sarah had suggested. As he worked, he imagined her smile and the way her eyes lit up when she talked about helping the kids. He paused, pen hovering over the page. Was he letting his growing attraction to her cloud his judgment?

"Focus, Michael," he muttered to himself. "This is about the kids, about the ministry."

But as he continued planning, he couldn't deny his excitement about working more closely with Sarah. The coffee meeting loomed large in his mind—an opportunity but also a potential complication.

As the first light of dawn crept through his window, Michael knelt by his bed and offered a prayer. "Lord, guide my steps. Help me to be the leader these kids need, to work alongside Sarah with integrity and purpose. And if there's something more here...if this connection is part of Your plan...give me the wisdom to navigate it in a way that honors You."

Rising, he felt a sense of peace settling over him. He picked up his phone, hesitating for a moment before typing a text to Sarah. *Great job yesterday! Coffee tomorrow at The Cozy Corner at 4?*

As he hit send, he felt nervousness but also anticipation. This coffee meeting could be the start of something new—for the ministry, for the kids, and perhaps for his heart as well.

Chapter 7

The Cozy Corner Café buzzed with the late afternoon crowd, the aroma of freshly brewed coffee and cinnamon rolls filling the air. As she'd gotten ready for school this morning after getting her text from Michael, she'd felt something significant was on the horizon. She'd said a quick prayer, "Lord, whatever You have planned, I'm ready. Guide my steps and open my heart."

Now she sat at a corner table, her fingers tracing the rim of her mug. She glanced at her watch for the third time in as many minutes. Michael was late.

As if summoned by her thoughts, the café door swung open, and he rushed in, his hair windswept and his cheeks flushed. "Sarah, I'm so sorry," he said, sliding into the seat across from her. "Youth group emergency. Tyler had a bit of a meltdown."

Sarah's heart clenched at the mention of the teen. "Is he okay?"

Michael ran a hand through his hair, his expression troubled. "Physically, yes. Emotionally...I'm not so sure. That's what I wanted to talk to you about."

As Michael ordered his coffee, Sarah had a feeling this conversation would test her commitment to the youth ministry. She said a silent prayer, "Lord, give me wisdom and compassion."

Michael leaned forward, his voice low. "Tyler's home situation is worse than we thought. His father's an alcoholic, and his mother...well, she's not really in the picture. He's been acting out at school, and I'm worried he might be experimenting with drugs."

Sarah's teacher instincts kicked in. "Have you considered reporting this to Child Protective Services?"

Michael nodded, his expression grim. "I've thought about it, but Tyler begged me not to. He's terrified of being put in foster care, of leaving his little sister behind. I just...I don't know what to do, Sarah. I feel like I'm failing him."

She reached out a hand, placing it over his without thinking. "You're not failing him, Michael. You're here, you care, and that means more than you know."

As their eyes met, Sarah felt a jolt of electricity run through her. She pulled her hand back, her cheeks flushed.

Michael cleared his throat, also looking flustered. "I, *uh*, I was hoping you might have some insight. You work with younger kids. Maybe you've dealt with similar situations?"

Sarah took a deep breath, pushing aside the lingering warmth from Michael's touch. "I have, unfortunately. It's never easy, but in my experience, the best thing we can do is create a safe space for Tyler. A place where he feels valued and heard."

As they brainstormed ideas, she was drawn into Michael's passion for helping these teens. His dedication was inspiring, and she felt her own resolve strengthen.

"What if we get started with the mentoring program we discussed?" she suggested. "Pair some older, more stable teens with the younger ones? It could give Tyler a sense of responsibility, something positive to focus on."

Michael's face lit up. "We should. Let's make plans and begin right away. This could work for many of our kids, not just Tyler."

As they fleshed out the details of the program, she noticed Michael's eyes crinkled when he smiled and the passion in his voice when he talked about the youth group. She pushed the thoughts aside, reminding herself this was a professional relationship.

"You know," Michael said, leaning back in his chair, "I've been thinking about Tyler's situation a lot. I wonder if there's a way we could involve his little sister in some of our programs too. Maybe if we could support the whole family, it would take some of the pressure off Tyler."

She nodded. "That's a great idea. We could start a program for siblings of our youth group members. It could be a safe space for them to connect with others in similar situations."

As they continued to brainstorm, she felt a growing sense of excitement. This was more than just youth ministry; they were creating a support network for entire families.

"Michael," she said, a thought occurring to her. "What if we partnered with local businesses? We could set up job training programs for parents like Tyler's dad. Maybe helping him find stable employment would address some of the root issues."

Michael's eyes widened. "Sarah, that's...that's incredible. You're really thinking big picture here."

She blushed at the compliment. "I just want to help. These kids and their families...they deserve a chance."

As the café began to empty, Michael glanced at his watch. "I can't believe how late it's gotten. Sarah, thank you. I don't know what I'd do without you."

The sincerity in his voice made her heart flutter. "That's what partners are for," she said, immediately regretting her choice of words. "I mean, ministry partners. Co-volunteers. You know what I mean."

Michael chuckled, his eyes twinkling. "I know exactly what you mean."

As they walked to their cars, excitement swirled inside her about the new mentoring program. But she was also concerned for Tyler and the other troubled teens. Then there was the undeniable attraction to Michael that she wasn't sure how to handle.

"Sarah," Michael said as they reached her car, his voice suddenly serious. "There's something else I wanted to talk to you about. The church is hosting a weekend retreat for the youth group next month. I was hoping you'd consider being a chaperone."

Her mind raced. A whole weekend with Michael and the teens? The thought was both thrilling and scary. "I'd love to," she heard herself say. "Just send me the details."

Michael's face broke into a wide grin. "Great! It'll be amazing, you'll see."

As she drove home, her mind was a whirlwind of thoughts. She'd come to the café expecting to discuss youth group activities and had left with a new mentoring program, a weekend retreat commitment, and a growing attraction to Michael she couldn't ignore.

Opening her Bible for her nightly devotion, a verse caught her eye.

"Trust in the Lord with all your heart and lean not on your own understanding; in all your ways submit to him, and he will make your paths straight." (Proverbs 3:5-6)

She took a deep breath, letting the words wash over her. "Okay, Lord," she whispered. "I'm trusting You with all of this. Guide my steps, my words, my heart."

The digital clock on Michael's dashboard blinked. 11:42 p.m. as he pulled into the church parking lot. He'd driven for hours after leaving the café, his mind darting from one set of thoughts and emotions to the next. Now, drawn by an inexplicable need for sanctuary, he found himself back where it all began.

As he entered the darkened cocoon of the church, the familiar scent of old hymnals and wooden pews enveloped him. Michael sank into a pew, his head in his hands. "Lord," he whispered, his voice echoing in the empty space, "what am I doing?"

The coffee meeting with Sarah had been more than he'd anticipated. Her passion for the kids, her innovative ideas—it all aligned so perfectly with his vision for the ministry. But the spark he'd felt when their hands touched, the way his heart raced when she smiled…it complicated things.

His gaze fell on the cross at the altar, its outline barely visible in the dim light. He thought of Tyler, of the countless other kids who depended on him for guidance. How could he balance his growing feelings for Sarah with his responsibilities to the youth group?

As if in answer, his phone buzzed with a text from Tyler. *Thanks for today, Pastor M. Sorry for freaking out. Can we talk tomorrow?*

Michael's heart contracted. Here was a reminder of the real stakes involved. These kids needed him to be fully present and fully committed. Could he do that if he was distracted by his feelings for Sarah?

Seeking guidance, he pulled out his pocket Bible. His gaze landed on a passage from 1 Corinthians. "Love is patient, love is kind. It does not envy, it does not boast, it is not proud. It does not dishonor others, it is not self-seeking, it is not easily angered, it keeps no record of wrongs."

The words spoke to him. Wasn't this the kind of love he felt called to show these kids? And maybe…maybe it was the kind of love that could strengthen his partnership with Sarah rather than complicate it.

With renewed clarity, he began sketching out plans for the mentoring program they'd discussed. As he worked, he imagined how Sarah's strengths could complement his own, how together they could create something truly impactful for the youth.

But a nagging doubt persisted. What if his personal feelings interfered with their professional relationship? Would pursuing something with Sarah jeopardize the very ministry they were so passionate about?

Michael knelt at the altar and offered a prayer. "Lord, guide my steps. Help me honor You in all I do and serve these kids with integrity and purpose. And Sarah…if this connection is part of Your plan, show me how to navigate it in a way that glorifies You."

As he rose, Michael felt a sense of peace. The path ahead wasn't clear, but he knew he wasn't walking it alone.

Driving home in the early hours of the morning, his mind was clearer than it had been in weeks.

He had a plan for Tyler, ideas for the mentoring program, and a determination to approach his relationship with Sarah—whatever it might become—with wisdom and faith.

Chapter 8

The school hallway echoed with the shuffle of feet and the slam of lockers as Sarah made her way to her classroom. Her mind was still buzzing from yesterday's coffee...meeting. Date? With Michael. As she turned the corner, she nearly collided with a small figure huddled by the water fountain.

"Lucy?" Sarah said, recognizing her student. "What are you doing out here, sweetie? The bell's about to ring."

Lucy looked up, her eyes red-rimmed and puffy. "I don't feel good, Ms. Thompson. Can I go home?"

Sarah's heart sank. She'd seen this before—a child using illness as an excuse to escape a difficult situation. Crouching down to Lucy's level, she asked, "What's going on, Lucy? You know you can talk to me."

Lucy's lower lip trembled. "The other kids...they were making fun of my clothes. They said I dress like a baby because everything's too small."

Sarah felt a surge of protective anger, followed by guilt. How had she not noticed Lucy's too-small clothes? She'd been so wrapped up in her life, the youth group, and...Michael.

"Oh, Lucy," Sarah said, pulling the girl into a hug. "I'm so sorry that happened. Those kids were wrong to say those things. But you know what? You are brave, kind, and so, so special. God made you exactly as you are, and He loves you more than you can imagine."

As Lucy sniffled against her shoulder, Sarah's mind raced. She needed to address this with the class to nip this bullying in the bud. But more than that, she needed to find a way to help Lucy and her mom.

Sarah thought of something that might help in situations like this. "Lucy, how would you like to help me with a special project?"

Lucy pulled back, wiping her eyes. "What kind of project?"

Sarah smiled. "Well, I was thinking about starting a clothing drive for families in need. We could collect used clothes and toys and maybe even have a big swap meet. What do you think?"

Lucy's eyes lit up. "Could I help with it?"

"Absolutely," Sarah said, her heart warming at Lucy's enthusiasm. "You'd be the perfect assistant for this project."

As they walked to class together, Sarah's mind was already whirring with plans. She'd need approval from the principal, coordinate with local charities, and maybe even reach out to Michael and the youth group for help...

The morning flew by in a blur of lessons and planning. During her lunch break, she dialed Michael's number before she could overthink it.

"Sarah?" Michael's voice was warm, sending a flutter through her stomach. "Everything okay?"

"Yes, I just...I had an idea I wanted to run by you," she said, feeling nervous. She explained the situation about Lucy and her plan for the clothing drive.

"That's fantastic, Sarah," Michael said, his voice filled with admiration. "The youth group would love to help out. This could be a great opportunity for our new mentoring program. We could pair some older teens with the elementary school kids to help organize the event."

As they brainstormed ideas, Sarah felt a familiar warmth spreading through her. Working with Michael like this, combining their passions and skills to help others, felt so natural, so right.

"Oh, before I forget," Michael said as they were wrapping up the call, "I wanted to let you know that Tyler's agreed to be part of the mentoring program. He's going to work with one of our middle schoolers."

Sarah's heart leaped. "Michael, that's wonderful! Do you think it'll help him?"

"I hope so," Michael said, his voice softening. "He needs to feel needed; you know? And, Sarah...thank you. For everything. I don't know what I'd do without you."

As she hung up, she felt a surge of joy at the progress they were making with the youth group. It felt so good. And the clothing drive was exciting. Doing something that really would help. She also couldn't deny the flutter in her heart at Michael's words.

The rest of the school day passed in a blur of activity. She met with the principal to get approval for the clothing drive, sent out emails to parents about the project, and started conjuring ideas to make the event fun and engaging for the whole school.

As she was packing up to leave, her phone buzzed with a text from Emma. *Wine and gossip at my place tonight? I want ALL the details about your coffee date with the hot youth pastor.* Her usual winking emoji at the end.

Sarah rolled her eyes but couldn't suppress a smile. *It wasn't a date! But...I'll be there at 7. There's a lot to talk about.*

That evening, as Sarah sat on Emma's couch, a glass of wine in hand, she ended up pouring out everything—her growing feelings for Michael, her excitement about the youth group and the new projects, and her concerns about Lucy and Tyler.

Emma listened, her expression a mix of excitement and concern. "Sarah," she said, "this all sounds amazing. But...are you sure you're not getting in over your head? I mean, between teaching, the youth group, this new clothing drive...when was the last time you did something just for you?"

Sarah opened her mouth to protest, then closed it again. Emma had a point. In her eagerness to help others, to follow what she believed was God's calling, had she neglected her own needs?

"I hear you," Sarah said. "But, Emma, this doesn't feel like work. It feels like...purpose. Like I'm where I'm supposed to be, doing what I'm supposed to do."

Emma smiled, reaching out to squeeze Sarah's hand. "I get it. Just...promise me you'll take care of yourself too, okay? And as for Michael..." Her eyes twinkled mischievously. "Girl, you've got it bad."

Sarah felt her cheeks flush. "I know. But we're just colleagues, friends at most."

"*Uh-huh,*" Emma said. "Just be careful, okay? Mixing work and romance can get complicated, especially when faith is involved."

As Sarah drove home, Emma's words echoed in her head, mixing with memories of Michael's smile, Lucy's tears, and Tyler's guarded expression.

She opened her Bible for her nightly devotion. "Love is patient, love is kind. It does not envy, it does not boast, it is not proud. It does not dishonor others, it is not self-seeking, it is not easily angered, it keeps no record of wrongs." (1 Corinthians 13:4-5)

She read the words over and over, letting them sink in. Was what she felt for Michael the start of love? Or just admiration for a colleague? And if it was love, what did that mean for their ministry work?

"Lord," she prayed, "I don't know where this path is leading. But I trust You. Guide my steps, guard my heart, and help me to love others the way You love me."

The next morning, she woke to a text from Michael. *Emergency youth group meeting tonight. Could really use your help. 7 pm at the church?*

Sarah's heart raced as she typed her reply. *I'll be there. Everything okay?*

Michael's response came quickly. *Not sure. Tyler's in trouble. Will explain more tonight. Thank you, Sarah.*

As she got ready for school, her mind was jumbled with worry for Tyler, and anticipation about seeing Michael. "Lord, whatever problems this day brings, help me to face them with Your strength and grace."

As she walked into her classroom, greeted by Lucy's bright smile and the excited chatter of her students about the upcoming clothing drive, Sarah felt a renewed vitality wash over her.

The day flew by in a blur of lessons, planning meetings for the clothing drive, and barely contained anticipation for the evening's youth group meeting. As the final bell rang, Sarah was rushing through her afterschool routine, her mind already at the church with Michael and the kids.

On her drive there, her phone rang.

"Hey, girl," Emma's voice came through the speakers. "Just checking in. How are you holding up with everything?"

Sarah sighed, grateful for her friend's concern. "I'm okay, Em. Busy, but good busy, you know? Actually, I'm on my way to an emergency youth group meeting now."

"Emergency?" Emma's voice sharpened with concern. "Sarah, are you sure you're not taking on too much? I mean, between teaching, the clothing drive, and now emergencies with the youth group..."

"I appreciate your concern, Emma, I really do," Sarah said, her voice firm but gentle. "But this feels right. It feels like where I'm supposed to be."

There was a pause on the other end of the line. "Okay," Emma said. "Just...be careful, all right? And call me if you need anything. Anytime."

As Sarah pulled into the church parking lot, she spotted Michael pacing outside, his brow furrowed. Her heart fluttered at the sight of him, but she pushed the feeling aside. There were more important things to focus on right now.

"Michael," she called as she got out of her car. "What's going on? Is Tyler okay?"

He ran a hand through his hair, his eyes troubled. "He got into a fight at school. It's bad. He's facing expulsion, and his dad...well, let's just say home isn't a safe place for him right now."

Sarah's heart faltered. "What can I do?"

Michael's eyes met hers, filled with gratitude and something else she couldn't name. "Just being here helps more than you know. Come on, the others are waiting inside."

As they walked into the church together, Sarah said a silent prayer, "Lord, give us wisdom. Help us be the support Tyler needs right now."

As they entered the youth room, filled with concerned kids and the palpable tension of worry, Sarah took a deep breath.

The church office felt claustrophobic as Michael paced, waiting for the last of the teens to be picked up. Tyler's words echoed in his mind. "You don't get it, Pastor M. No one does." The boy's pain had been palpable, his anger a thinly veiled cry for help. And now, with expulsion looming and his home situation deteriorating, Michael felt the weight of responsibility pressing down on him like never before.

A soft knock interrupted his thoughts. Sarah stood in the doorway; concern etched on her face. "Everyone's gone. How are you coping?"

He ran a hand through his hair, struggling to find the right words. "I don't know. I feel like I'm failing these kids. Tyler, especially. How did I not see this coming?"

Sarah stepped into the office, her presence a calming force. "You can't blame yourself, Michael. We're doing our best."

"But is our best good enough?" The question hung in the air, heavy with implication.

Seeking guidance, Michael reached for his Bible, letting it fall open. His gaze landed on a passage from Isaiah. "So do not fear, for I am with you; do not be dismayed, for I am your God. I will strengthen and help you; I will uphold you with my righteous right hand."

The words sparked something in Michael. He turned to Sarah, an idea growing. "What if we create a crisis intervention plan? Something that addresses not just the spiritual needs of our kids, but their practical needs too?"

Sarah's eyes lit up, and he felt a familiar warmth spread through him. Together, they began outlining a comprehensive support system—mentorship programs, counseling resources, and emergency housing options.

As they worked, Michael marveled at how in sync they were. But with that realization came a wave of uncertainty. Were his growing feelings for her clouding his judgment? Was he leaning on her too much, too soon?

"Michael?" Sarah's voice broke through his thoughts. "You, okay? You seemed lost for a moment there."

He forced a smile. "Just thinking about the next steps, I can't tell you how much I appreciate your help. But...are you sure it's not too much? Between your teaching, the clothing drive, and now this..."

Sarah's expression softened. "This is where I'm meant to be. I feel it in my soul."

Her words mirrored his own sense of calling. As they finished their plan, he felt a tinge of something—a connection with Sarah that both thrilled and terrified him.

Locking up the church, he said a silent prayer, "Lord, guide us in this. Show us how to be there for these kids and how to navigate this partnership You've blessed us with. And if there's something more here...help me to honor it in a way that glorifies You."

As he drove home in the quiet of the night, Michael's mind raced with possibilities and potential pitfalls. The crisis with Tyler illuminated gaps in their ministry but also highlighted the strength of his partnership with Sarah. Whatever lay ahead, he felt ready to face it.

He felt such a heart full of love for the kids he served. Now, he also had the support of someone who understood his calling as deeply as he did.

He pulled into his driveway and held onto the hope that God was working all things together for good, even in the midst of crisis his guidance was always there.

Chapter 9

The church parking lot was a flurry of activity as Sarah helped load the last of the camping gear into the van. Nervous excitement bubbled up in her chest. The youth group retreat was here, and with it, a weekend of close quarters with Michael and the teens. Turning to grab another sleeping bag, she saw Tyler hanging back from the group, his posture tense and guarded.

"Hey, Tyler," Sarah said, keeping her tone casual. "Want to give me a hand with these sleeping bags?"

Tyler shrugged but made his way over. As they worked side by side, Sarah could sense the tension radiating off him. She said a quick prayer, "Lord, give me the words to reach him."

"You know," she said, "I used to hate these kinds of trips when I was your age. Being away from home, surrounded by people I didn't know well...it was frightening."

Tyler glanced at her, surprise flickering in his eyes. "Yeah?"

Sarah nodded. "Yeah. But you know what? They ended up being some of the best experiences of my life. They taught me that I was stronger than I thought, and that God was with me, even when I felt alone."

Tyler was quiet for a moment, then mumbled, "I don't know if I believe in all that God stuff."

Sarah's heart faltered, but she kept her voice steady. "That's okay. Doubt is a normal part of faith. What matters is that you're here, giving it a chance."

As they finished loading the van, Michael approached, his face breaking into a warm smile, probably at the sight of them working together. "Great job, team! We're just about ready to hit the road."

Sarah noticed Tyler's slight relaxation in Michael's presence. It was clear that the youth pastor had already made an impact on the troubled teen.

As the group gathered for a pre-trip prayer, Sarah stood next to Michael. The closeness of his presence sent a flutter through her stomach. She chided herself for the reaction. This weekend was about the kids, not her growing feelings for Michael.

The drive to the campsite was filled with the chatter and laughter of excited kids, punctuated by the occasional burst of song. She was drawn into conversations about school, relationships, and faith, marveling at the openness and vulnerability of these young people.

As they neared the campsite, Michael said from the driver's seat, "Alright, team! We're almost there. Remember, this weekend is about growing closer to God and to each other. Let's make it count!"

The enthusiasm in his voice was contagious, and she felt her own excitement building. This was why she'd gotten involved in youth ministry—to make a difference in these kids' lives, to help them see the love and purpose God had for them.

As they pulled into the campsite, the reality of the weekend ahead hit Sarah. Three days in the wilderness with a group of hormonal teenagers and the man she was trying hard not to fall for. What could possibly go wrong?

The first situation presented itself as they began setting up tents. It became clear that they were one tent short. Sarah overheard two girls whispering and giggling, and her teacher's instincts kicked in.

"All right, what's going on?" she asked, approaching the girls.

One of them, a redhead named Amber, looked up with a mischievous glint in her eye. "Oh, nothing. We were just wondering where you and Pastor Michael would sleep."

Sarah felt her cheeks flush. "We'll figure something out," she said. "Now, how about you two help Tyler and Jake with their tent? They seem to be having some trouble."

As she walked away, Sarah caught Michael's eye across the campsite. He raised an eyebrow in question, and she shook her head slightly, mouthing, "Later." They had bigger issues to deal with right now.

The tent situation was resolved, with Sarah volunteering to share with the female chaperone, and Michael bunking with the other male youth leader. Crisis averted, but Sarah couldn't ignore the feeling that this was just the first of many issues they'd face this weekend.

As the group gathered for their first campfire of the trip, she was seated next to Tyler. The firelight flickered across his face, highlighting the weariness in his eyes.

"How are you doing with everything?" Sarah asked.

Tyler shrugged. "It's okay, I guess. Different from what I'm used to."

Sarah nodded, understanding the unspoken weight behind his words. "Different can be good sometimes. It gives us a chance to see things from a new perspective."

As Michael began the evening's devotional, Sarah watched Tyler's face. He seemed to be listening, even if his expression remained guarded.

Michael's warm and passionate voice carried across the campfire. "Tonight, I want to talk about trust—trusting in God, trusting in each other, and learning to trust ourselves. It's not always easy, especially when life has given us reasons to be cautious. But trust is the foundation of any meaningful relationship—with God and each other."

As he spoke, Sarah reflected on her own journey of trust. She now trusted in her calling to youth ministry, and she was accepting the connection she felt with Michael. She knew God had a plan for all of this.

The devotional led to a group discussion, and Sarah was impressed by the depth and honesty of the teens' responses. Even Tyler contributed, albeit minimally, by sharing a story about a time he'd had to trust a friend in a difficult situation.

As the night wore on and the kids drifted off to their tents, Sarah lingered by the fire with Michael. The crackling flames cast a warm glow over his features, and she felt her heart skip a beat.

"You were great tonight," she said. "It was amazing how you connected with the kids and got them to open up."

Michael smiled, the firelight dancing in his eyes. "I couldn't have done it without you, Sarah. The way you are with them, especially Tyler...you have a gift."

Their eyes met, and for a moment, Sarah felt the world fall away. It was just the two of them, the fire and the vast starry sky above. She opened her mouth to speak, not sure what she was going to say, when a crash and a yelp from one of the tents shattered the moment.

"Duty calls," Michael said with a rueful smile, standing up. "We should make sure no one's staging a midnight raid on the snack supply."

As they made their way to the source of the commotion, Sarah offered a silent prayer of thanks—for the interruption, yes, but also for this moment, this place, and the growing certainty that she was where she was meant to be.

The tent incident was a clumsy attempt at a practical joke, easily resolved with a firm but gentle reminder about respect and safety. As Sarah crawled into her sleeping bag that night, her mind jumped from one thought and feeling to another.

She'd come to this retreat to help guide the youth and be a positive influence in their lives. Her mind was racing, and she felt on a deep level that this weekend might end up changing her just as much as it changed them.

The campfire embers glowed as Michael made his final rounds of the campsite. The rhythmic sound of sleeping teenagers filled the air, a contrast to the turmoil in his own mind. As he approached his shared tent, he paused, his eyes drawn to the soft light from Sarah's tent.

A familiar voice whispered, "You're getting too close, Michael. Remember what happened last time."

He shook off the thought, but the memory lingered—another retreat, another co-leader, and a lapse in judgment that had nearly cost him his ministry. He'd vowed never to let his personal feelings interfere with his calling again. But Sarah...she was different. Wasn't she?

As if summoned by his thoughts, she emerged from her tent, a flashlight in hand. "Can't sleep either?" she whispered; her smile visible even in the dim light.

Michael felt his heart race. "Just doing a final check," he managed. "Everything okay?"

She nodded, then hesitated. "Actually...I'm a bit worried about Tyler. He seemed so closed off during the devotional."

The mention of Tyler snapped Michael back to reality. This was why they were here—for the kids, not for his own confused feelings.

"I noticed that too," he said, grateful for the distraction. "I've been thinking...what if we paired him with Jake for tomorrow's trust exercises? Jake's been making real progress lately, and his positivity might rub off on Tyler."

Sarah's eyes lit up, and Michael felt a familiar warmth. "That's brilliant, Michael. And maybe we could..."

As they talked about ways to reach Tyler and the other struggling teens, Michael loved how Sarah's ideas dovetailed in perfectly with his own. It was exhilarating and alarming all at once.

Their planning session was interrupted by a rustling from one of the tents. Amber, who'd caused a stir earlier, poked her head out. "Pastor Michael? Ms. Thompson? I...I think I heard something in the woods. Like, big something."

Michael and Sarah exchanged a glance. "I'll check it out," Michael said. "Sarah, can you stay with Amber?"

As Michael ventured into the darkness, flashlight in hand, he said a silent prayer, "Lord, guide my steps. Help me to be the leader these kids need, to work alongside Sarah with integrity and purpose. And if there's something more here—if this connection is part of Your plan—give me the wisdom to navigate it in a way that honors You."

The "big something" was nothing more than a raccoon rummaging through an improperly secured trash bag. As Michael returned to camp, he felt his direction become clearer. Approaching the campsite, he saw Sarah sitting with Amber, the two giggling. The sight warmed his heart, reminding him of the real reason they were here—to connect with these kids, to show them God's love in action.

"All clear," he announced. "Just a hungry raccoon."

As they settled Amber back into her tent, Michael caught Sarah's eye. The moonlight illuminated her face, and for a moment, he was struck by how right this felt—working together, supporting these kids, sharing this calling.

"We make a good team," Sarah whispered as they parted ways.

Michael nodded, not trusting himself to speak. His mind and heart were racing as he settled into bed. He'd come to this retreat to guide the youth and be a positive influence in their lives.

But as he drifted to sleep, he knew this weekend would bring about changes for everyone. He slept, wrapped in the peace of knowing he was where God wanted him to be, doing what he was called to do.

Chapter 10

The morning sun filtered through the tent fabric, casting a warm glow over the sleeping campers. Sarah stirred, her mind slowly coming into focus. The events of the previous night came rushing back—the campfire, the deep conversations, the moment with Michael by the fire. She felt a flutter in her stomach that had nothing to do with hunger.

As she emerged from her tent, she was greeted by Michael preparing breakfast over the campfire. He looked up, a smile spreading across his face that made her heart skip.

"Good morning, sunshine," he said. "Sleep well?"

Sarah was about to respond when a commotion from the boys' tent area caught their attention. Tyler burst out, his face a mask of anger and hurt, followed by Jake, one of the other teens.

"I told you to stay out of my stuff!" Tyler shouted; his fists clenched at his sides.

Sarah and Michael exchanged a quick glance before moving to intervene. This was the challenge they'd been preparing for—helping these teens navigate conflict and emotions in a healthy way.

"Whoa, hold on there," Michael said, his voice calm but firm. "What's going on, guys?"

Jake, looking sheepish, held up a small book. "I just wanted to borrow Tyler's journal for the writing activity. I didn't think it was a big deal."

Tyler's face flushed with anger and embarrassment. "It is a big deal! That's private!"

Sarah stepped in. "Jake, I know you didn't mean any harm, but it's important to respect other people's privacy. Tyler, I understand you're upset, but let's take a deep breath and talk this through calmly."

As they worked through the conflict, Sarah noticed the way Michael handled the situation. His patience, his ability to listen without judgment, the way he guided the boys to a resolution—it was all so natural, so genuine.

Once the situation was defused and the boys had made their apologies, Sarah pulled Tyler aside. "Are you okay?" she asked.

He shrugged; his eyes fixed on the ground. "I guess. It's just...that journal is the only place I can be honest about everything. About my dad, about...stuff."

Sarah nodded, understanding the weight behind his words. "It's good that you have an outlet, Tyler. Writing can be therapeutic. Have you ever thought about sharing some of what you write with others? Maybe in a group like this?"

Tyler looked up, surprise and fear flashing across his face. "I don't know if I could do that."

"You don't have to decide now," Sarah reassured him. "But sometimes, sharing our burdens can make them lighter. And you might be surprised by how many people understand what you're going through."

Tyler nodded and walked away. Sarah felt a presence behind her. She turned to find Michael, who had an admiration-filled look on his face.

"You're amazing with them, you know that?" he said.

Sarah felt a blush creep up her cheeks. "I'm just trying to help. Like you do."

Michael shook his head. "It's more than that. You have a gift, Sarah. The way you connect with these kids, the way you see right to the heart of their struggles...it's special."

Their eyes met, and Sarah felt that familiar spark of connection. She allowed herself to imagine what it would be like to work alongside Michael like this all the time, to build a life and a ministry together.

The moment was broken by the sound of sizzling bacon, reminding them of the hungry teens waiting for breakfast. As they moved to finish preparing the meal, Sarah said a silent prayer of gratitude for this opportunity, for these kids, and for the growing certainty that this was where she belonged.

The day unfolded with a series of team-building activities and nature hikes. She was amazed by the teens' resilience and depth. Watching them open up, support each other, and grapple with big questions about faith and life was inspiring.

She walked beside Michael during a quiet moment on the trail. The forest around them was peaceful, and the filtered sunlight created an almost magical atmosphere.

"Can I ask you something?" she asked softly.

Michael nodded, his eyes curious.

"How did you know? That this was what you were meant to do with your life?"

Michael was quiet for a moment, his brow furrowed in thought. "I'm not sure I ever had one big 'aha' moment," he said. "It was more like a series of small realizations. Every time I worked with kids, every time I saw someone's faith grow or watched them overcome an obstacle...it just felt right. Like I was where I was supposed to be."

She nodded, understanding all too well. "I think I'm starting to feel that way too," she admitted. "Being here, working with these kids...it feels like purpose."

Michael's face broke into a warm smile. "I'm glad you're here, Sarah. Not just for the kids, but..." he trailed off, his eyes meeting hers with an intensity that made her breath catch.

Before either of them could say more, a shout from up ahead broke the moment. They hurried to catch up with the group, but Sarah could feel the weight of unspoken words between them.

The afternoon brought more activities, including a trust fall exercise that pushed many kids out of their comfort zones. She watched with pride as Tyler, after much hesitation, allowed himself to fall backward into the waiting arms of his peers.

As the sun began to set, the group gathered once again around the campfire. Michael led them in a discussion about the day's experiences, encouraging them to share what they'd learned about trust, teamwork, and faith.

She listened, her heart full, as one teen after another opened up about their struggles and triumphs. When it was Tyler's turn to speak, she held her breath, hoping he'd find the courage to share.

"I, *uh*," Tyler began, his voice shaky. "I want to read something. From my journal." He glanced at Sarah, who gave him an encouraging nod. "It's about my dad and...stuff."

As he read, his words were raw and honest, and Sarah felt tears pricking her eyes. She watched the other teens' reactions and saw the dawning understanding and empathy on their faces. This, she realized, was what it was all about: creating a safe space for vulnerability, growth, and healing.

When Tyler finished, there was a moment of profound silence. Then, one by one, the other teens began to share their own stories and struggles. The atmosphere around the campfire transformed into one of deep connection and support.

As the night wore on and the kids began to head to their tents, she found herself once again by the fire with Michael. The weight of the evening's emotions hung in the air between them.

"Thank you," Michael said, "for encouraging Tyler to share. I've been trying to get through to him for too long, and you managed it in such a short time."

Sarah shook her head. "It wasn't me. It was God working through all of this—through you, through the other kids. I'm just grateful to be a part of it."

Michael reached out, taking her hand in his. The touch sent a jolt through her body. "You're more than just a part of it, Sarah. You're essential. To the kids, to the ministry, to..." he trailed off, his eyes searching hers.

Her heart raced. She knew they were on the edge of something profound, something that might change things. But before either of them could speak, a scream shattered the night air.

They jumped up, racing toward the source of the sound. As they approached the girls' tent area, Sarah's mind raced with possibilities. Was someone hurt? Had there been an animal sighting?

What they found was both a relief and a new situation. Two girls were in a heated argument, tears streaming down their faces. Sarah and Michael worked to calm the situation. She felt both frustrated at the interruption of her moment with Michael, but also gratitude for the reminder of why they were here.

After they settled the girls and headed back to their tents, Michael caught her hand. "We should talk," he said. "Tomorrow?"

She nodded, her heart fluttering. "Tomorrow," she agreed.

Lying in her sleeping bag that night, her mind was a whirlwind of thoughts and feelings. The growth she'd seen in her kids, the deepening of her own faith, and the undeniable connection she felt with Michael were all intertwined in ways she hadn't anticipated.

She fell asleep with a prayer on her lips, asking for guidance, wisdom, and the strength to face tomorrow's challenges.

The question hung in the air, heavy with Tyler's pain and doubt. Michael felt a familiar ache in his chest—the desire to have all the answers warring with the humility of knowing he didn't.

"That's a tough one, Tyler," Michael admitted, choosing his words. "I wish I could tell you there's a simple answer, but faith...it's not always easy."

He paused, searching for the right words. "You know, there's a verse in Hebrews that says, 'Faith is confidence in what we hope for and assurance about what we do not see.' Sometimes, believing that God is listening, that He's working even when we can't see it—that's the hardest part of faith."

Tyler nodded; his brow furrowed in thought. "But how do you hold onto that when everything feels so...messed up?"

He felt a surge of compassion for the young man beside him. How many times had he wrestled with the same questions?

"For me," he said, "it helps to remember when I've seen God work. The moments of unexpected grace, the strength I've found when I thought I had nothing left. And it helps to have people around me who can remind me of God's faithfulness when I struggle to see it myself."

As they continued to talk, Michael opened up about his own journey of faith—the doubts he'd faced, the moments of clarity, the ongoing process of trusting God even in the midst of uncertainty.

By the time Tyler returned to his tent, a glimmer of hope that hadn't been there before was in his eyes. As Michael watched him go, he felt a renewed faith in his calling. This—walking alongside these young people as they wrestled with life's big questions—was why he'd become a youth pastor.

But with that realization came a sobering thought. The depth of need these teens had, the complexity of their struggles—it was more than he could handle alone. He thought of Sarah, of the natural way she connected with the kids, and how together they made a stronger unit.

Michael's heart raced as he allowed himself to imagine a future where they led this ministry together—not just as colleagues but as partners in every sense of the word. The idea thrilled and terrified him.

Pulling out his pocket Bible, Michael flipped it open, and it landed on a familiar passage. "Two are better than one, because they have a good return for their labor: If either of them falls down, one can help the other up." (Ecclesiastes 4:9-10)

The words seemed to leap off the page, speaking to his current situation. He closed his eyes, offering up a prayer.

"Lord, I think I'm falling for Sarah. If this is Your will, show me how to move forward in a way that honors You, her, and this ministry. And if it's not...give me the strength to let go."

As the last embers died out, he returned to his tent, his mind in overdrive, and his heart beating wildly. The problems they faced were daunting, but for the first time, he allowed himself to hope for something more—a partnership that could strengthen their ministry and maybe lead to a deeper personal connection.

He zipped up his sleeping bag, wrapped in the peace of faith, deepening with each new challenge and the warmth of a love that was steadily blooming.

Chapter 11

The morning mist clung to the campground, casting an ethereal glow over the sleeping tents. Sarah zipped up her jacket, her breath visible in the cool air as she made her way to the campfire.

Her mind hopped from thought to thought from the previous night—Tyler's breakthrough, the deepening connections among the kids, and that moment with Michael by the fire. As she approached, she saw Michael already there, stoking the flames. Their eyes met, and Sarah felt a flutter in her stomach that had nothing to do with the early hour.

"Good morning," Michael said, his smile warm despite the chill in the air. "Sleep well?"

She was about to respond when a commotion from the boys' tent area caught their attention. They exchanged a worried glance before hurrying over. As they approached, Tyler stumbled out of his tent, his face pale and his body shaking.

"Tyler?" Michael called out, sounding concerned. "What's wrong?"

Tyler looked up, his eyes wide with fear. "I don't feel good. I think...I think I need to go home."

Sarah's heart sank. After yesterday's progress, this felt like a significant setback. She prayed, "Lord, give us wisdom to handle this."

Michael helped Tyler to a nearby log, and she knelt before him. "Tyler, can you tell us what's going on? Are you feeling sick?"

Tyler shook his head, his voice gentle and faint. "No, it's not that. I just...after last night, sharing all that stuff...I feel exposed. Like everyone knows my secrets now."

Sarah's heart ached for the boy. She glanced at Michael, seeing her own concern mirrored in his eyes.

"Tyler," Michael said, "what you did last night was incredibly brave. You opened up and allowed others to see the real you. That's not easy, but it's an important part of growth and healing."

Sarah nodded, adding, "And remember how the others responded? They shared their own struggles too. You're not alone in this, Tyler."

Other teens began to emerge from their tents, drawn by the commotion. Sarah watched as several of them, including Jake, approached.

"Is everything okay?" Jake asked, his eyes darting between Tyler and the adult leaders.

Michael looked at Tyler, asking permission. When Tyler nodded, Michael explained the situation to the group.

What happened next brought tears to Sarah's eyes. One by one, the kids stepped forward, sharing words of encouragement and support for Tyler. Jake apologized again for the journal incident, telling Tyler how much he admired his courage in sharing.

Sarah felt a hand on her shoulder. She turned to find Michael standing close, his eyes shining with emotion.

"This," he said, "is why we do what we do."

She nodded, unable to speak past the lump in her throat. At that moment, she felt a surge of certainty about her calling to youth ministry and the importance of this work.

As the group began to disperse for breakfast preparations, Tyler approached Sarah and Michael. His eyes were red-rimmed, but his gaze was steady.

"I think...I think I want to stay," he said. "If that's okay."

She felt her heart swell with pride. "Of course, it's okay, Tyler. We're so glad you're here."

As he walked away, she turned to Michael. "We need to talk," she said, her voice low. "About last night, about...us."

Michael nodded, his expression serious. "You're right. After breakfast? We can take a walk while the kids are doing their morning devotionals."

She agreed, her stomach churning with anticipation and nervousness. As they moved to join the group for breakfast, she couldn't shake the feeling that this conversation would change things.

The morning passed in a blur of activity—breakfast, clean-up, and getting the teens started on their devotionals. Sarah walked alongside Michael on a secluded trail, the sounds of the camp fading behind them.

The weight of their unspoken words hung between them. Michael broke the silence.

"Sarah," he began, his voice soft but intense, "I can't ignore what's happening between us. The connection we have and how we work together with the kids feels like more than just a professional relationship."

Sarah's heart raced. She took a deep breath, steadying herself. "I feel it too, Michael. But I'm scared. What if pursuing this jeopardizes our ministry? What if it doesn't work out, and we can't work together anymore?"

Michael stopped walking and turned to face her. His gaze met hers, filled with a mix of emotions that made Sarah's breath catch.

"I can't promise it won't be complicated," he said. "But I believe that God brought us together for a reason. The way we complement each other in ministry and the impact we're having on these kids together. I think it's worth exploring."

Sarah felt tears pricking at her eyes. She wanted to give in to these feelings, to see where this connection with Michael might lead. But the responsibility they held—to the youth group and to their ministry—weighed heavily on her.

"Can we...can we take it slow?" she asked, her voice low and hushed. "Figure out what this means for us and for our ministry?"

His face broke into a warm smile. He reached out, taking her hand in his. "Of course. We'll navigate this together, with prayer and wisdom."

As they stood there, hands clasped and hearts full, Sarah said a silent prayer of gratitude for this moment, for Michael, and for the clarity she felt about her calling.

Their peaceful moment was shattered by the sound of shouting from the direction of the camp. They exchanged a worried glance before hurrying back, hands dropping apart as they focused on the potential crisis ahead.

As they emerged from the trail, they found the camp in chaos. Two groups of teens argued, with Tyler caught in the middle, looking overwhelmed and ready to bolt.

Sarah's heart sank. They'd made so much progress, and now it felt like they were right back where they started. As she and Michael moved to intervene, she wondered if this setback was a sign—a reminder of the problems they'd face if they pursued a relationship while trying to lead this ministry together.

But as they worked to calm the situation, Sarah drew strength from Michael's steadfastness beside her.

They defused the conflict among the kids, but Sarah felt the tension of their newly acknowledged feelings hanging in the air. As they prepared for the afternoon's activities, she was aware of the delicate balance between their feelings and their responsibilities to the youth group.

The sun dipped below the tree line, casting long shadows across the campground. Michael stood at the edge of the clearing, watching the teens settle around the campfire for the evening devotional. His mind raced, replaying the day's events—the conversation with Sarah, the argument among the kids, the constant balancing act between his feelings and his responsibilities as a youth pastor.

A familiar voice cut through his thoughts. "Pastor Michael? Can I talk to you for a sec?"

He turned to see Jake; his face etched with worry. Michael nodded and led them to a quiet spot away from the group.

"What's on your mind, Jake?"

The boy hesitated, then blurted out, "I think Tyler's planning to run away. I overheard him talking to someone on his phone about getting picked up tonight."

Michael's heart felt heavy. Just when they thought they'd made progress, another crisis loomed. He thanked Jake for the information, then sought out Sarah, pulling her aside to share the news.

"What do we do?" she whispered; her eyes wide with concern. "If we confront him, he might bolt. But we can't just let him leave."

Michael ran a hand through his hair, feeling the weight of the decision. This wasn't just about Tyler anymore—it was about the trust they'd built with all the kids, about the integrity of their ministry.

"We pray," Michael said finally. "And then we talk to him. Together."

As they approached Tyler, who sat alone at the edge of the group, Michael said a silent prayer, "Lord, give us the words. Help us reach him."

"Tyler," Michael began, "we need to talk."

The conversation that followed was tense, emotional, and transformative. Tyler broke down, admitting his fears about returning home and facing his father. Sarah and Michael listened, offering support and practical solutions.

"What if we set up a meeting with your dad?" Michael suggested. "All of us together. We can be there for you, help mediate."

Tyler looked up, a glimmer of hope in his eyes. "You'd do that?"

"Of course," Sarah said. "You're not alone in this, Tyler. We're here for you—all of us."

As Tyler rejoined the group, looking more at peace than he had all weekend, Michael caught Sarah's eyes. Their connection crackled with intensity, probably born from their shared purpose and the difficulty they'd overcome.

Later, as the teens drifted off to their tents, Michael sat alone by the dying fire. He pulled out his Bible, seeking guidance. "I can do all things through Christ who strengthens me." (Philippians 4:13)

The words took on new meaning in light of the day's events. He and Sarah had faced a significant issue in their fledgling relationship and ministry, and they'd come through it stronger and more united in their purpose.

But as he closed the Bible, a new worry gnawed at him. How would they maintain this balance once they returned to Oakbrook? How would their relationship impact their work with the youth group and their standing in the church?

He offered another prayer, his voice scarcely audible over the crackling embers, "Lord, show us the way forward. Help us to honor You in all we do—in our ministry and in our hearts."

As he zipped himself into his sleeping bag, he held onto the peace that came from knowing they would face whatever lay ahead—with faith, with purpose, and with a love that was deepening with every shared challenge.

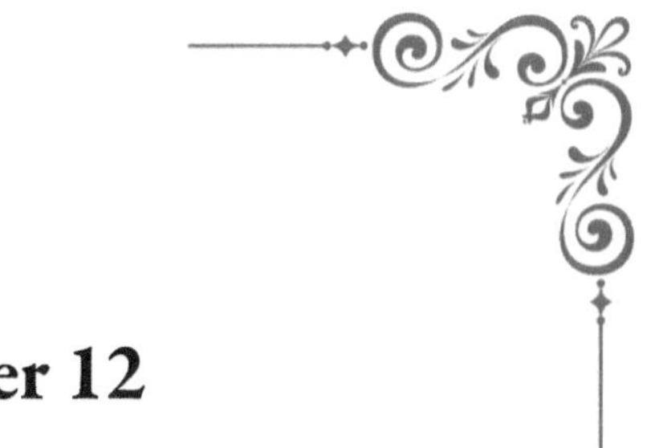

Chapter 12

The afternoon sun beat down on the campground, the earlier mist long burned away. Sarah wiped the sweat from her brow as she helped set up the team-building exercises. Her mind drifted back to her conversation with Michael, the warmth of his hand in hers, the promise of something more. She shook her head, forcing herself to focus on the task. The kids needed her full attention, especially after the morning's drama.

As they gathered for instructions, Sarah noticed the lingering tension among some of the teens. Tyler, in particular, seemed on edge, his eyes darting between his peers. Sarah prayed, "Lord, help us bring these kids together. Show us how to heal these rifts."

Michael stepped forward to explain the first activity—a complex puzzle that required the entire group to work together to solve. As he spoke, Sarah watched the teens' reactions. Some looked excited, others skeptical, and a few, including Tyler, seemed downright resistant.

"Alright, team," Michael said, his voice carrying across the clearing. "This is about more than just solving a puzzle. It's about learning to work together and to value each person's unique contributions. Everyone has a role to play here."

As the activity began, Sarah and Michael circulated among the kids, offering guidance and encouragement. With Tyler hovering on the outskirts, Sarah was drawn to the struggling group.

"Hey, guys," she said, approaching them. "How's it going over here?"

Amber sighed in frustration. "We can't figure this part out. And Tyler won't even try to help."

Sarah glanced at Tyler, seeing the hurt and defensiveness flash across his face. She took a deep breath, praying for the right words.

"Tyler," she said, "I remember you mentioning that you enjoy puzzles. Do you see anything here that the others might have missed?"

Tyler hesitated, then moved closer to the group. After studying the puzzle pieces, he pointed to a section. "I think...I think this part goes here," he said.

To everyone's surprise, Tyler's suggestion was the key to unlocking that puzzle section. As the group's excitement grew, Sarah watched Tyler's posture relax, a small smile tugging at the corners of his mouth.

Throughout the afternoon, Sarah and Michael worked to create opportunities for cooperation and understanding among everyone. With each successful obstacle overcome, the earlier tensions seemed to fade, replaced by a growing sense of camaraderie.

As the final activity wound down, Sarah stood beside Michael, watching the kids laugh and chat.

"We make a good team," Michael said, his hand brushing against hers.

She felt a flutter in her stomach at the touch. "We do," she agreed, her voice just as low. "But, Michael, we need to be careful. The kids have to come first."

He nodded, his expression serious. "You're right. We'll take it slow and keep things professional around the kids. But, Sarah..." he trailed off, his gaze meeting hers with an intensity that made her breath catch. "I want you to know that this—us—it means something to me. Something important."

Before she could respond, Jake, one of the teens, ran up to them and interrupted.

"Pastor Michael, Ms. Thompson!" he said. "We were thinking...could we have a special campfire tonight? Like, a talent show or something?"

Sarah and Michael exchanged a glance, it was a great opportunity for further bonding among the group.

"That's a great idea, Jake," Sarah said, smiling. "Why don't you and some of the others start organizing it? Michael and I will help with whatever you need."

As Jake ran off to spread the news, Michael turned to Sarah. "A talent show, *huh*? Think we should show off our own hidden talents?"

Sarah laughed, grateful for the moment of levity. "I don't know about you, but my talents are best left hidden. Though I might be persuaded to join in if it'll encourage the kids."

As they began to prepare for the evening's festivities, Sarah liked the progress they'd made with the teens, and the deepening connection with Michael but she had a lingering concern about how to balance it all.

The campfire talent show turned out to be a highlight of the trip. Kids who had been shy and reserved at the beginning of the weekend now performed skits, sang songs, and even showcased impressive magic tricks.

Sarah teared up as Tyler, with Jake's encouragement, got up to read a poem he had written. The raw honesty of his words and the supportive reactions from his peers were a testament to how far they'd all come in just a few short days.

As the night wore on, Michael stood up to address the group. "I'm so proud of all of you," he said, his voice warm with emotion. "The courage, creativity, and kindness you've shown tonight—and throughout this trip—was truly inspiring."

He paused, his gaze finding Sarah's in the firelight. "Ms. Thompson and I have a little surprise for you. We've decided to extend our trip by one day. Tomorrow, instead of heading home, we'll go to town to volunteer at the local food bank."

The announcement was met with excited chatter from the kids—discussing ideas about how they could help—their enthusiasm infectious.

As everyone drifted off to their tents, Sarah settled once again by the fire with Michael. The crackling flames cast a warm glow over his features, and she felt her heart contract.

"That was a great idea," she said. "The volunteer work, I mean. It'll be good for them to put their newfound teamwork skills to use helping others."

Michael nodded, his eyes never leaving hers. "I thought so, too. And...I thought it might give us more time together, away from our usual routines."

She felt a blush creep up her cheeks. "Michael..."

He reached out, taking her hand in his. "I know, I know. We're taking it slow. But Sarah, being here with you and working with these kids together feels right. Like this is where we're meant to be."

She squeezed his hand, her heart full. "I feel it too," she admitted. "I'm just...I'm scared of messing this up. The ministry, the kids, us..."

His thumb traced gentle circles on the back of her hand. "We'll figure it out together," he said. "With faith, patience, and each other."

As they sat there, hands intertwined and hearts open, she prayed a silent prayer of gratitude for this moment and the growing certainty that this was where God wanted her to be.

Their peaceful moment was interrupted by muffled sobs from one of the tents, growing louder by the second. With a worried glance between them, they hurried to investigate.

They found Amber curled up in her sleeping bag, tears streaming down her face. As Sarah knelt beside her, she was struck by how young and vulnerable the confident teen looked.

"Amber, sweetie, what's wrong?" Sarah asked.

Between sobs, Amber managed to choke out, "I...I just got a text from my mom. My parents are getting a divorce."

Sarah's heart hurt for her. She looked up at Michael, seeing her own concern mirrored in his eyes. Navigating this crisis would require all their compassion, wisdom, and faith.

As they worked to comfort Amber and decide how to handle this situation with the rest of the group, it felt good to help these young people, pointing them toward faith and hope.

They sat outside Amber's tent long into the night, offering comfort and support. As the dawn light began to break over the campsite, she exchanged a look of understanding with Michael.

The first rays of dawn painted the sky in soft pink and gold as he returned to his tent. His body ached from the long night spent comforting Amber, but his mind was wide awake, churning with thoughts and feelings.

As he reached for the tent zipper, a rustling sound caught his attention. Tyler emerged from his tent; his face etched with concern.

"Is Amber okay?" he asked.

Michael nodded, impressed by Tyler's empathy. "She will be. It's going to take time, but she's strong. And she has all of us to support her."

Tyler hesitated, then blurted out, "My parents split up too. A couple of years ago. It...it sucks."

The raw honesty in Tyler's voice struck Michael. Here was an opportunity—and a challenge. How could he help these kids navigate such personal pain while maintaining appropriate boundaries?

"Tyler," Michael said, "would you be willing to talk to Amber? Share your experience. Sometimes, it helps to know you're not alone."

The boy's eyes widened, fear crossing his face. "I...I don't know what to say."

Michael placed a gentle hand on Tyler's shoulder. "Just be honest. Share your story. And remember, this isn't about fixing her problems. It's about being there for her."

Tyler determinedly nodded before heading toward Amber's tent, and Michael said a silent prayer, "Lord, guide their words. Help them find strength and comfort in each other."

Michael turned to find Sarah watching the exchange, a soft smile on her face. "You handled that beautifully," she said, standing beside him.

Her presence both calmed and exhilarated him. He took a deep breath, wrestling with the growing feelings in his heart. "Sarah, about last night...about us..."

She held up a hand, her expression a mix of tenderness and caution. "I know. We need to talk. But right now, these kids need us to be fully present."

He nodded, admiring her wisdom and dedication. "You're right. But later?"

"Later," Sarah agreed, her hand squeezed his.

As they began preparing for the day ahead, his mind raced with plans. The food bank volunteer work must be adjusted to accommodate Amber's emotional state. And how could they use this situation to teach the group about empathy, support, and faith during difficult times?

He pulled out his Bible, seeking guidance. A verse from Romans stood out. "And we know that in all things God works for the good of those who love him, who have been called according to his purpose."

He felt those words. Maybe this crisis, painful as it was, could be an opportunity for growth for everyone.

The teens began to stir, and Michael gathered them for a morning devotional. He spoke about community and bearing one another's burdens, careful not to reveal Amber's personal situation.

"Today," he concluded, "as we go to serve at the food bank, I want us to remember that everyone we meet has their own struggles. Our job is not to fix them, but to show them God's love through our actions."

The teens nodded, a new depth of understanding in their eyes. Michael caught Sarah's gaze across the group, seeing his own mix of pride and concern reflected there.

Michael overheard snippets of conversation—kids offering words of encouragement to Amber, sharing their own stories of family struggles. His heart swelled with pride at their growth, even as he recognized the delicate balance needed.

Chapter 13

The morning sun filtered through the trees, casting dappled shadows across the campground. Sarah stood at the edge of the clearing as everyone packed their gear. Her gaze was drawn to Amber, who moved slowly, her usual vivaciousness dimmed by the news of her parents' divorce.

Watching Michael busily loading the van, she felt a familiar flutter in her stomach. The events of the past few days—their growing closeness, the issues they'd faced together—swirled in her mind.

Suddenly, a shout broke through her reverie. She turned to see Tyler, his face contorted with anger, squaring off against Jake.

"I told you to leave me alone!" Tyler yelled; his fists clenched at his sides.

Sarah's heart raced as she hurried toward the boys, praying for wisdom. "What's going on here?" she asked, calmly but firmly.

Jake, looking sheepish, held up Tyler's journal. "I was just trying to return it. I thought...after the talent show, maybe we could talk about writing sometime."

Tyler's face flushed with anger and embarrassment. "I don't want to talk about it. Not with you, not with anyone!"

As Sarah tried to defuse the situation, she saw Michael approaching. Their eyes met, and a silent communication passed between them. They'd made so much progress with Tyler and all the kids, but this outburst threatened to undo it all.

"Tyler," Michael said, "I know you're overwhelmed. But lashing out isn't the answer. Remember what we discussed—using our words, not our fists?"

Tyler's shoulders slumped, the fight seeming to drain out of him. "I just...I thought things were getting better. But now, going back home..." he trailed off, his eyes filling with tears.

Sarah's heart ached for this poor kid. She glanced at Michael, seeing her own concern mirrored in his eyes. They'd known this moment would come—when the reality of returning to their everyday lives would hit the kids hard.

"Why don't we take a walk?" Sarah suggested, placing a gentle hand on Tyler's shoulder. "Just you and me. We can talk about what's worrying you."

As they moved away from the group, Sarah prayed, "Lord, give me the words to reach him. Help me be a light in his darkness."

Their conversation was raw and honest. Tyler opened up about his fears of returning home, facing his alcoholic father, and losing the sense of belonging he'd found at the retreat. Sarah listened, her heart breaking for this young man who'd already faced so much.

"Tyler," she said, "I want you to know something. What you've experienced here—the connections you've made, the strength you've found—that doesn't disappear when we leave this place. God's love and our support go with you."

As they talked, Sarah shared her experiences of facing difficult times and finding strength in her faith when everything else seemed uncertain. She watched as Tyler's posture relaxed, a glimmer of hope returning to his eyes.

When they returned to the group, she was relieved that Michael had things under control. Everyone was gathered in a circle, engaged in what looked like a final devotional before their departure.

As Sarah and Tyler joined the group, Michael caught her eye, a question in his gaze. She gave a small nod, signaling that things were okay. The warmth of his answering smile sent a flutter through her.

The devotional, led by Michael, focused on integrating the retreat's lessons and experiences into their everyday lives. Sarah watched the teens' faces as Michael spoke—determination, hope, and, yes, some apprehension.

"Remember," Michael said, his voice carrying across the clearing, "what we've built here isn't limited to this place. The connections you've made, the growth you've experienced—that goes with you. And so does God's love."

As the group bowed their heads for a final prayer, tears caught in Sarah's throat. It was beautiful and humbling to witness.

After the prayer, it was time to board the van for their trip into town. As the kids loaded up, Sarah pulled Michael aside.

"How's Tyler?" he asked, concern evident.

Sarah sighed. "He's struggling with the idea of going home. I think... I think we need to consider involving child services when we get back."

Michael nodded, his expression grave. "I was thinking the same thing. We'll need to handle it carefully, but Tyler's safety has to come first."

As they discussed their plans, she was struck by how in sync they were and how naturally they worked together. This thrilled and terrified her.

"Michael," she said, "about us...I think we need to talk. Really talk. About what this means for our ministry, for the kids."

His eyes met hers, filled with understanding and something deeper that made her heart race. "You're right. After we finish today's volunteer work and get the kids home safely, let's make time to talk—just the two of us."

She nodded, equally nervous and excited at the prospect. As they boarded the van, she silently prayed, "Lord, guide us. In our ministry, in our relationship, in all of it. Help us to serve You and these kids to the best of our abilities."

The drive into town was filled with the chatter of excited teens, punctuated by moments of quiet reflection. Sarah constantly checked on Amber and Tyler, worried about how they were coping.

They pulled up to the food bank. Sarah felt pride in them for their willingness to serve, but also concern for those struggling. It was hard watching them go through this turmoil. And humming in the background, was the undeniable excitement about her evolving relationship with Michael.

As they unloaded from the van, she caught sight of a familiar face that made her blood run cold. Standing at the entrance of the food bank was none other than Tyler's father, his disheveled appearance and unsteady gait suggesting he was already intoxicated despite the early hour.

Her gaze met Michael's, a silent message passing between them. The complications they'd anticipated had arrived sooner than expected and with higher stakes than they'd imagined. How they handled the next few moments could have far-reaching consequences for Tyler.

Taking a deep breath, Sarah steeled herself for the problem ahead. "Lord," she prayed, "give us strength and wisdom. Help us protect these kids and show Your love, even in this difficult moment."

Sarah placed a protective hand on Tyler's shoulder, feeling the boy's body tense as he too, caught sight of his father.

The day that had started with such promise now teetered on the edge of crisis, and Sarah knew that every decision, every word, would be crucial.

Chapter 14

The tension in the air was palpable as they all approached the food bank entrance. Tyler's father swayed, his bloodshot eyes narrowing as he caught sight of his son.

"Tyler!" he slurred. "What're you doing here? Thought you were on some church trip."

Sarah felt Tyler stiffen under her hand. She exchanged a quick glance with Michael, who nodded imperceptibly before stepping forward.

"Mr. Scott," Michael said, his voice calm but firm. "I'm Michael Carter, the youth pastor at Oakbrook Community Church. We're here to volunteer at the food bank as part of our retreat."

Tyler's father squinted at Michael, then let out a harsh laugh. "Church, *huh*? Filling my boy's head with all that religious nonsense?"

Sarah's heart ached as she saw Tyler shrink back, the confidence he'd gained over the weekend seeming to evaporate in his father's presence. She prayed, "Lord, give us wisdom to handle this situation."

Michael, to his credit, remained composed. "Sir, we're here to help our community. Perhaps you'd like to join us? Many hands make light work, as they say."

It seemed like the situation might be defused. Then Tyler's father took an unsteady step forward, his face contorting with anger.

"Don't patronize me, preacher man," he spat. "Tyler, get over here. We're going home."

Sarah felt a surge of protective instinct. "Mr. Scott," she said, stepping forward. "Tyler is in our care for the duration of this trip. We'll make sure he gets home safely this evening."

The man's gaze swung to Sarah, his eyes narrowing. "And who are you? His new mommy?"

The venom in his voice made Sarah flinch, but she stood her ground. "I'm Sarah Thompson, a teacher and youth group volunteer. We're all here to support Tyler and help our community."

As the confrontation unfolded, she was aware of the other teens watching, their expressions of fear and concern. She caught Amber's eye, seeing the girl's own family troubles reflected in her worried gaze.

Just when it seemed the situation couldn't get tenser, the food bank manager emerged from the building, drawn by the commotion.

"Is everything alright out here?" she asked, her eyes darting between the group and Tyler's father.

Michael seized the opportunity. "Yes, ma'am. We're the volunteer group from Oakbrook Community Church. We were just about to come in and get started."

The manager nodded, though her expression remained wary. "All right then, come on in. Mr. Scott," she added, turning to Tyler's father, "I think it's best if you come back another time."

Sarah thought he might argue. But something in the manager's tone seemed to deflate him. He shot one last glare at Tyler before stumbling away, muttering.

As they filed inside, Sarah could feel the weight of what had just transpired settling over the group. She and Michael exchanged a look, there was a lot to address.

"Alright, everyone," Michael said, his voice steady despite the tension. "Let's focus on why we're here today. We can serve our community and make a real difference."

As the manager began assigning tasks, Sarah pulled Tyler aside. "Are you okay?"

He nodded, though, his eyes remained downcast. "I'm sorry," he mumbled. "I didn't know he'd be here."

Sarah's heart broke for the young man. She cupped the boy's cheeks. "Tyler, look at me," she said. When he met her gaze, she continued, "You have nothing to be sorry for. What happened out there...that's not on you. You're so much stronger than you realize."

As they rejoined the group, Sarah noticed how the other teens rallied around Tyler. Jake, in particular, stayed close to his side, offering quiet words of encouragement as they worked.

Throughout the morning, Sarah checked on the teens while trying to process her own emotions about what had happened. Her concern for Tyler warred with her growing certainty that they needed to involve child services. And underlying it all was a deepening appreciation for Michael's steady presence and leadership.

They took a lunch break, and Michael pulled Sarah aside. "We need to talk about Tyler," he said, his voice low. "After what happened this morning..."

She nodded, her heart heavy. "I know. We can't in good conscience send him back to that situation. But, Michael, if we report this, it could damage his trust in us. In the whole youth group."

He ran a hand through his hair, the frustration evident. "I know. But his safety has to come first. We have a duty of care, both legally and morally."

As they discussed their options, Sarah loved how connected they were and how well they worked together to tackle problems. It was scary but also uplifting, realizing how deeply she'd come to rely on Michael's partnership.

"Whatever we decide," Sarah said, "we're in this together."

Michael's gaze met hers, filled with warmth and something deeper that made Sarah's heart race. "Always," he said, reaching out to squeeze her hand.

The moment was interrupted by a crash from the main room, followed by raised voices. They rushed back to find Tyler and Jake in a heated argument, a toppled box of canned goods scattered at their feet.

"I don't need your pity!" Tyler shouted, his face flushed with anger and embarrassment.

Jake, looking hurt and confused, held up his hands. "It's not pity, man. I'm just trying to be your friend."

Sarah and Michael exchanged a quick glance before moving to intervene. As they worked to defuse the situation and clean up the mess, Sarah felt they were at a crucial turning point. The progress they'd made with Tyler and all the kids seemed fragile.

As the day wore on, she mediated conflicts, offered encouragement, and tried to keep the focus on their volunteer work. Michael's steady support offered a balm to her frayed nerves.

By the time they finished their shift, everyone was exhausted, physically and emotionally. As they loaded back into the van for the trip home, she felt relief. But also, apprehension. They'd made it through a tough day, but the real test was yet to come.

"Michael," she said as they prepared to leave, "what are we going to do about Tyler?"

His expression was grave as he met her gaze. "We'll need to talk to Pastor David as soon as we return. And...I think we need to make that call to child services tonight."

Sarah nodded, her heart heavy but certain. "You're right. It won't be easy, but it's the right thing to do."

As they drove back to the church, the van was unusually quiet, and Sarah found her mind racing. The day's events had brought into sharp focus the complexities of their ministry and the weight of responsibility they carried.

She prayed, "Lord, guide us. In our ministry, in our decisions, in our hearts. Help us to serve You and these kids to the best of our abilities."

Pastor David was waiting for them as they pulled into the church parking lot. His serious expression suggested that their difficulties were far from over.

Michael turned to her, his eyes reflecting the same mix of determination and apprehension she felt. "Ready?" he asked.

She took a deep breath. "Ready."

Whatever came next, they would face it—as partners in ministry, and she allowed herself to hope as something more. The road ahead would have its potholes and pitfalls, but as they exited the van, ready to face the next hurdle, she felt a burst of energy and purpose. The complications might be rising, but so was her faith in the path God had set before them.

The church office, as always, felt claustrophobic as Michael paced, waiting for Pastor David to finish his phone call. The weight of the day's events pressed heavily on his shoulders—Tyler's father's appearance, the tension among the teens, and the looming decision about involving child services. He paused at the window, watching Sarah comfort Tyler in the parking lot, her gentle presence a balm to the troubled boy.

A memory flashed through Michael's mind—himself at Tyler's age, torn between loyalty to his struggling father and the desperate need for help. He shook off the thought as Pastor David hung up the phone.

"Michael," the older man said, his voice grave. "The board's caught wind of the situation. They're...concerned about potential liability issues."

Michael felt his stomach drop. "Liability? We're trying to help a kid in crisis, not avoid a lawsuit."

Pastor David sighed, rubbing his temples. "I know that, and you know that. But not everyone sees it that way. There's talk of implementing new policies and stricter guidelines for the youth ministry."

The implications hit Michael like a physical blow. New policies could mean less flexibility and less ability to respond to the unique needs of kids like Tyler. How could they maintain the heart of their ministry while navigating these new issues?

"What do we do?" Michael asked, his voice barely a whisper.

Pastor David met his gaze, his eyes kind but firm. "We pray. We make our case to the board. And we trust that God has a plan in all of this."

Michael nodded, reaching for his Bible. It fell open to a familiar passage in James. "Consider it pure joy, my brothers and sisters, whenever you face trials of many kinds because you know that the testing of your faith produces perseverance."

With today's events, it took on new meaning. Was this a test of their faith? Of their calling to ministry?

As Michael pondered this, he got an idea. What if they could use this situation as an opportunity to educate the board about the real issues facing their youth and push for more comprehensive support systems within the church?

Energized by this new perspective, Michael began outlining a proposal. A series of workshops for church leaders, testimonies from youth who had overcome obstacles, and maybe even a community outreach program specifically aimed at struggling families.

A soft knock interrupted his thoughts. Sarah stood in the doorway, concern and determination on her face. "How'd it go?"

Michael felt a surge of gratitude for her presence. "It's complicated," he admitted. "But I think...I think we might have an opportunity here."

As he shared his ideas, Michael watched Sarah's eyes light up. Her enthusiasm and insight added depth to the plan.

"Michael," Sarah said as they finished, "whatever happens with the board, with Tyler...we've got this."

He reached for her hand, feeling the now-familiar spark at her touch. "Yeah, you're right," he replied, his voice thick with emotion.

They walked toward the waiting group of kids and joined them. Their faces held determination and apprehension. As they explained the situation and their plans for the future, he couldn't help feeling they were on the verge of something monumental—a crisis that would either strengthen their ministry or break it apart. However, he was ready to take that leap into the unknown.

Chapter 15

The church office felt suffocating, the air tense as Sarah and Michael sat across from Pastor David. The ticking of the wall clock seemed loud in the silence that followed their report of the day's events. Sarah's gaze darted to Michael, his strength beside her.

Pastor David leaned back in his chair; his brow furrowed. "You're certain about this? Calling CPS for Tyler?"

Sarah took a deep breath, steeling herself. "We are, Pastor. After what we witnessed today...we can't in good conscience send him back to that situation."

Michael nodded in agreement. "We have a duty of care, both legally and morally. Tyler's safety has to come first."

The pastor's gaze moved between them, his expression unreadable. "I understand your concerns, but have you considered the potential fallout? This could damage Tyler's trust in us, in the entire youth ministry."

Sarah felt a flicker of doubt but pushed it aside. "We've considered that, Pastor. But we believe that in the long run, this is what's best for Tyler."

As they continued to discuss the situation, Sarah was glad she and Michael were presenting a united front.

Just as it seemed they had Pastor David convinced, a knock at the door interrupted them. The church secretary poked her head in, her expression apologetic. "I'm sorry to interrupt, but Tyler's father is here. He's...well, he's quite insistent on speaking with you all."

Sarah's heart sank. She exchanged a worried glance with Michael, seeing her own concern mirrored in his eyes. This was the moment of truth, the confrontation they'd been dreading.

As Tyler's father burst into the office, his face flushed with anger and the smell of alcohol clinging to him, Sarah said a prayer, "Lord, give us strength and wisdom to handle this situation."

What followed was a tense and heated exchange. Tyler's father alternated between angry accusations and tearful pleas, insisting that they had no right to interfere in his family's life.

"You don't understand," he slurred, his bloodshot eyes darting between them. "Tyler needs me. I'm all he's got left."

Sarah's heart ached at the pain in the man's voice, even as she recoiled from his aggressive demeanor. She glanced at Michael, seeing the conflict in his eyes that she knew must be mirrored in her own.

It was Pastor David who broke the impasse. "Mr. Scott," he said, his voice firm but compassionate, "we all want what's best for Tyler. But right now, what's best for him is to be in a safe environment. Let us help you both."

For a moment, it seemed like Tyler's father might lash out. But then, something in Pastor David's tone seemed to reach him. His shoulders slumped, the fight draining out of him.

"I...I don't know how to fix this," he admitted, his voice scarcely audible.

Pastor David began to discuss options for counseling and support, and Sarah felt a wave of relief. They had made the right decision, difficult as it was.

She turned to Michael, found his hand, and squeezed it. The warmth of his touch grounded her.

As the meeting concluded and arrangements were made for Tyler's temporary placement in a safe home, Sarah felt relief that Tyler would be safe but also sadness for his family's brokenness. It was such a lot to take on for a young kid. And she felt the overwhelming weight of responsibility they carried in their ministry too.

Later, as she and Michael walked to their cars, Sarah finally felt the emotional toll of the day. Tears welled up in her eyes.

"Hey," Michael said, pulling her into a gentle embrace. "You did good today. We did good."

Sarah nodded against his chest, soaking in the comfort from his warmth. "I just hope we made the right choice. For Tyler, for all the kids."

Michael pulled back, his gaze meeting hers with an intensity that made her breath catch. "We did what we believed was right, Sarah. That's all we can do. Trust in God to handle the rest."

As they stood in the dimly lit parking lot, she felt the shift in the air between them. The shared problems and the emotional intensity of the day had brought their feelings for each other into focus.

"Michael," she began, her voice hesitant. "I think we need to talk. About us."

He nodded, hope and apprehension in his eyes. "You're right. But not here, not now. We both need some time to process everything that's happened."

Sarah agreed, even as a part of her longed to stay in this moment with him. "Tomorrow? We could meet for coffee and talk things through."

Michael smiled, the warmth of it reaching his eyes. "It's a date. Or...you know what I mean."

As they parted ways, Sarah felt instinctively that they were on the edge of something life changing. Their ministry, their relationship, their individual faiths—all of it seemed to be converging in ways she never could have anticipated.

Driving home, Sarah's mind raced with the events of the day and the possibilities of tomorrow. She prayed, "Lord, guide us. In our ministry, in our hearts. Help us to serve You and these kids to the best of our abilities and to navigate whatever path You've set before us."

She pulled into her driveway, and her phone buzzed with a text from Emma. *Heard about what happened with Tyler. You, okay? Wine and talk tomorrow night?*

Sarah smiled, grateful for her friend's support. *Thanks, Em. It's been a day. And...raincheck on the wine? I have plans tomorrow evening.*

Emma's response was immediate. *Plans? With a certain handsome youth pastor, perhaps?* Her usual suggestive emoji. *Spill the tea, girl!*

Sarah laughed, shaking her head. She'd fill Emma in later. For now, she needed rest and reflection.

She got ready for bed and opened her Bible, finding comfort in the familiar words of Proverbs 3:5-6, "Trust in the Lord with all your heart and lean not on your own understanding; in all your ways submit to him, and he will make your paths straight."

Sarah took a deep breath, letting the words wash over her. Whatever tomorrow brought—in her ministry or relationship with Michael—she would trust in God's plan.

The streetlights flickered to life as Michael pulled into his driveway, his mind still reeling from the day's events. He sat in his car, unable to bring himself to go inside just yet. The weight of the decision they'd made about Tyler, the intensity of the confrontation with his father, and the lingering warmth of Sarah's embrace in the parking lot—created a maelstrom of emotions he couldn't quite untangle.

A text alert broke through his reverie. It was from Tyler. *Thanks for everything, Pastor M. I'm scared, but I think this is for the best.*

Michael's heart clenched. The boy's courage in such upheaval was inspiring and heartbreaking. As he typed out a reassuring reply, a memory surfaced—himself at Tyler's age—wishing someone had been brave enough to intervene in his family's dysfunction.

With a sigh, Michael made his way inside. His apartment felt eerily quiet after the chaos of the day. He moved to his study, drawn to the familiar comfort of his books and Bible. But as he reached for his copy of Scripture, his gaze fell on a framed photo on his desk—his ordination day, Pastor David beaming proudly beside him.

A wave of doubt washed over him. Had they overstepped today? Would their actions help Tyler or drive him away from the church—from God?

Seeking guidance, Michael opened his Bible, letting it fall open where it would. "Learn to do right; seek justice. Defend the oppressed." (Isaiah 1:17)

The words resonated with him, seeming to affirm their decision. But with that affirmation came a new worry. How would this situation affect their ministry moving forward? And what about his feelings for Sarah?

As if conjured by his thoughts, his phone buzzed with a text from her. *Can't sleep. Keep thinking about today, about tomorrow. You, okay?*

Michael smiled, warmth spreading through his body. *Better now. Looking forward to our talk.*

Setting down his phone, he knelt by his bed, praying. "Lord, guide us in this. Show us how to help Tyler and how to strengthen our ministry. And Sarah...if this connection is part of Your plan, help me navigate it with wisdom and integrity."

He rose and felt a sense of peace settling over him. The situations ahead were daunting. This was why he'd been called to ministry—to make a real difference in people's lives, to be a tangible expression of God's love.

Moving to his desk, he began outlining a proposal for the church board—a comprehensive plan for supporting at-risk youth and their families. As he worked, he knew Sarah's insights and strength would enhance the program.

The realization thrilled and scared him. Their partnership in ministry was evolving into something deeper, something that could either strengthen their work or complicate it beyond measure.

The dawn light began to creep through his window, and he crawled into bed, exhausted but hopeful. Whatever lay ahead—he knew they would face them, with faith as their guide. He drifted to sleep, wrapped in the peace of knowing he was where God wanted him to be, doing what he was called to do.

His alarm blared, jolting him awake. He reached to silence it. His gaze fell on the coffee shop receipt from his last meeting with Sarah, tucked into his Bible as a makeshift bookmark.

With nervous anticipation, he began to prepare for the day ahead, knowing that the conversation this evening could change his life.

Chapter 16

The Cozy Corner Café buzzed with the afternoon crowd, the aroma of freshly brewed coffee filling the air. Sarah sat at a corner table, her fingers tracing the rim of her mug. She glanced at her watch, then at the door, her heart racing with anticipation.

As if summoned by her thoughts, Michael walked in, his gaze scanning the room before landing on her. The warmth of his smile sent a flutter through her stomach.

"Hey," he said, sliding into the seat across from her. "How are you doing?"

Sarah took a deep breath, steadying herself. "I'm okay. It's been…a lot to process. How about you?"

Michael nodded, his expression serious. "Same here. I spoke with Tyler's temporary guardians this morning. He's safe but struggling to adjust."

As they caught up on the developments with Tyler's situation, Sarah noticed their easy rapport, the natural way they balanced each other's strengths and concerns.

Finally, Michael set down his coffee cup, his gaze meeting hers with an intensity that made her breath catch. "Sarah, about us…I think it's time we talk about what's happening here."

She nodded, her heart racing. "You're right. This…whatever it is between us, it's affecting our ministry, our decisions."

"Is that such a bad thing?" Michael asked. "The way we work together and balance each other out makes us stronger leaders who are better equipped to help these kids."

Sarah felt a little hope at his words, but caution held her back. "I feel that too, Michael. But what if it doesn't work out? What happens to our ministry then?"

He reached across the table, taking her hand in his. The warmth of his touch sent a jolt through her. "Sarah, I can't promise that it will be easy. But I believe that God brought us together for a reason. I think the connection we have and the way we work together in ministry are worth exploring."

They delved into their feelings, fears, and hopes, and happiness swept over Sarah at the mutual attraction and respect they shared. Even though the fear of the unknown was there, the overwhelming sense of God's presence helped.

Their conversation was interrupted by the buzz of Michael's phone. His expression grew serious as he read the message.

"It's Pastor David," he said, looking up at Sarah. "There's been a development with Tyler's case. His father...he's agreed to enter a rehab program."

Sarah's eyes widened. "That's...that's wonderful news, isn't it?"

Michael nodded, but his expression remained cautious. "It is. But it also complicates things. The church has been asked to play a role in supporting Tyler, his sister, and his father through this process."

As they discussed the implications of this new development, Sarah felt like they were being tested. Their budding romantic feelings, commitment to the ministry, and individual faiths—all of it was converging.

"Michael," Sarah said, "whatever we decide about ourselves, we need to put the ministry first. These kids need us to be fully present and fully committed."

He squeezed her hand, his eyes full of understanding and something deeper that made Sarah's heart race. "You're right. But, Sarah, I don't think it has to be an either-or situation. I believe we can explore this connection between us while still honoring our commitment to the ministry."

As they worked through their concerns and hopes, Sarah felt a growing sense of peace. This wouldn't be easy, but with faith and mutual respect, could they navigate this new territory?

As they were wrapping up their conversation, Sarah's phone buzzed with a text from Emma. *Emergency at the school. Lucy's mom collapsed. She's asking for you.*

Sarah's heart contracted. She looked up at Michael, seeing the concern in his eyes as she relayed the message.

"Go," he said. "I'll handle things with Pastor David. We'll talk more later."

As she rushed out of the café, her mind whirling with worry for Lucy and her mother, she wondered if this was another test of her commitment to her students and her ability to balance her personal life with her calling.

She said a quick prayer as she drove, "Lord, give me strength and wisdom. Help me be there for Lucy and all these kids who need support."

Arriving at the school, she found Lucy in the nurse's office, her small frame racked with sobs. She gathered the distraught child in her arms and felt the weight of responsibility settling on her shoulders.

"It's going to be okay, sweetie," she murmured, stroking Lucy's hair. "Everything is going to be alright."

As she comforted Lucy and worked with the school administration to handle the situation, Sarah's mind drifted back to her conversation with Michael. It gave her strength in this moment of crisis.

Hours later, after ensuring that Lucy's mother was receiving proper medical care and making arrangements for Lucy's temporary care,

Sarah had a moment to breathe. She pulled out her phone to find several missed calls and texts from Michael.

His latest message read, *I'm just checking in. How are you doing? I'm here if you need anything.*

Sarah felt a wave of gratitude. This—this unwavering support, this shared commitment to their calling—was what mattered.

It's been a tough day, but Lucy's safe, and her mom's getting help. Can we talk later? I think I've made a decision about us.

Michael's response was immediate. *Of course. I'll be here whenever you're ready.*

As she drove home that evening, emotionally and physically exhausted, she felt clarity settling over her. The difficulties of the day—supporting Tyler's family and being there for Lucy in crisis—had sharpened her focus on what mattered in her life and ministry.

"Thank you, Lord, for Your guidance. Thank you for bringing Michael into my life and for calling me to serve these kids. Help me to honor Your plan in all that I do."

Sarah knew that the conversation awaiting her with Michael would be pivotal. But for the first time since their feelings for each other had become clear, she felt at peace with the path forward.

As she pulled into her driveway, she caught sight of a familiar figure sitting on her front porch. Michael stood as she approached, his eyes filled with concern and something deeper that made her heart skip.

"I hope you don't mind," he said. "I just...I needed to see that you were okay."

Sarah felt tears welling up in her eyes, overwhelmed by the events of the day and the depth of care in Michael's gesture. Without a word, she stepped into his embrace, drawing strength from his presence. They stood there in the growing twilight. Sarah knew that whatever lay ahead—they would face them with faith as their guide.

Sitting on her porch swing, they talked late into the night, discussing their feelings and fears and shared their commitment to their calling.

When they parted ways, Sarah felt hope. They'd chosen to move forward together, balancing their sprouting relationship and their dedication to the youth ministry.

She wondered how they would navigate the complexities of a romantic relationship within their professional roles? How would the church community, the kids, and their colleagues respond? These questions lingered, but she'd face it with faith and love.

Michael closed Sarah's front door behind him and felt a stormy mix of joy and apprehension. As he walked to his car, a text alert broke the late-night stillness from Pastor David. *There will be an emergency board meeting at 7 a.m. It will discuss Tyler's situation and the youth ministry.*

His stomach clenched. The timing couldn't be worse. How could he face the board, knowing his relationship with Sarah had shifted so dramatically?

He drove home to get some sleep, and his thoughts raced. The board had been skeptical about their handling of Tyler's case. Would this new development with Sarah compromise their credibility? More importantly, how could they balance their personal relationship with their professional responsibilities?

His sleep was fitful but as he arrived at the church the next morning, Michael paused in the parking lot, seeking guidance. Above the entrance, the etched verse called to him. "For I know the plans I have for you," declares the Lord, "plans to prosper you and not to harm you, plans to give you hope and a future." (Jeremiah 29:11)

The familiar words took on new meaning. Whatever difficulties lay ahead, Michael felt this path—with Sarah in ministry—was part of God's plan.

Entering the boardroom, he was met with a sea of serious faces. Pastor David spoke first, his tone grave. "Michael, the board has concerns about recent events. There's talk of restructuring the youth ministry, possibly bringing in outside leadership."

The words hit Michael like a physical blow. Everything they'd built, the progress they'd made with kids like Tyler—it all hung in the balance.

Taking a deep breath, Michael addressed the board, speaking of the transformations they'd witnessed and the lives they'd touched. He outlined plans for expanding their outreach, including the mentoring program he and Sarah had discussed.

As he spoke, he felt a familiar presence. He turned to see Sarah slipping into the room, her eyes meeting his with unwavering support. It helped. He continued, his voice growing more confident.

"I understand your concerns," he said. "But I believe that what's happening in our youth ministry—the connections we're forming, the support we're providing—is what these kids need. What our community needs."

He paused, then decided to take a leap of faith. "My relationship with Sarah has deepened. But I believe this strengthens our ministry. Our shared commitment and our skills make us better equipped to serve these kids."

The room fell silent. Michael held his breath, aware of the weight of this moment.

Finally, one of the board members spoke. "I've seen the change in my grandson since he started attending your youth group. Whatever you're doing, it's working."

Others began to nod, the atmosphere in the room shifting. Pastor David's expression softened. "Perhaps we've been too hasty. Michael, Sarah—why don't you prepare a more detailed proposal for expanding the youth ministry? We'll reconvene next week to discuss it."

As the meeting adjourned, Michael felt relief and anticipation. They'd won a reprieve, but the real work was just beginning.

"I hope you don't mind that I came," said Sarah. "I felt like I needed to be here."

Michael took her hand, it felt natural in his. "I'm glad you were. We're in this together, right?"

She nodded, her eyes shining. "Together."

The path ahead wouldn't be easy but as they walked to their cars, an overwhelming drive ignited within him.

They parted ways, each heading to their responsibilities. Michael started his car, and his phone buzzed. Tyler.

Can we talk? I need your help.

The message reminded him of the real stakes in their ministry and the lives they're committed to impacting.

Chapter 17

The church fellowship hall buzzed as Sarah helped Michael hang the last decorations for the youth group's end-of-summer celebration. Their hands brushed as they reached for the same streamer, sending a familiar jolt through Sarah's body. She caught Michael's eye, seeing her own joy and nervousness reflected there.

It had been two months since they'd decided to pursue a relationship while continuing their work in the youth ministry. So far, they'd managed to keep things professional at church, but tonight's event would be their first major test—a gathering of not just the youth group but their families as well.

As if on cue, Pastor David walked in, his eyebrows perhaps raising at the sight of Sarah and Michael standing so close. "Everything ready for tonight?" he asked, his tone neutral.

Sarah stepped back, straightening her shirt. "Just about, Pastor. We're expecting a good turnout."

Michael nodded. "We've got some great activities planned. And Tyler's agreed to share his testimony."

At the mention of Tyler, Pastor David's expression softened. The teen's progress over the summer—along with his father's commitment to rehab— had been a source of hope for the entire church community.

"That's wonderful," Pastor David said. "But...are you sure he's ready? It's a big step, sharing something so personal."

Sarah and Michael exchanged glances, their unspoken communication a sign of their deepening bond. "We've talked it through with him," Sarah explained. "He feels it's important to share his story, to maybe help others who are struggling."

Pastor David nodded, though, Sarah could see a flicker of concern in his eyes. "Alright. Just...be prepared. Sometimes, these things can stir up more emotions than we anticipate."

As the pastor left, Sarah felt a knot of anxiety forming in her stomach. She turned to Michael, seeing her own worries mirrored in his expression. "Do you think we're doing the right thing?" she asked. "Encouraging Tyler to share like this?"

Michael took her hand and squeezed it. "We've prayed about this, Sarah. We've prepared Tyler as best we can. Now we need to trust in God's plan."

Sarah nodded, Michael's touch and unwavering faith gave her strength. As they finished the preparations, she said a prayer, "Lord, guide us tonight. Help us to support these kids and their families, to be a light in their lives."

The evening started well, with families trickling in and the air filled with laughter and conversation. Sarah's heart swelled as she watched Lucy proudly introduce her mother—now recovered and beaming—to the other parents.

As the program began, Sarah and Michael took turns leading games and activities. Their natural rapport and shared enthusiasm were infectious. Sarah noticed the approving smiles from some of the parents and a few raised eyebrows at their obvious connection.

Finally, it was time for Tyler's testimony. As the teen made his way to the front, Sarah felt her heart racing. She caught Michael's eye across the room, and his steady gaze grounded her.

Tyler's voice was shaky at first but grew stronger as he shared his story, the pain of his mother's abandonment, his father's struggle with alcoholism, and the hope he'd found through the youth group and his faith.

"I didn't think anyone could understand what I was going through," Tyler said, his eyes glistening with unshed tears. "But Ms. Thompson and Pastor Michael...they showed me that I wasn't alone. That God hadn't forgotten me."

Sarah felt her own eyes welling up, overwhelmed by the impact their ministry had had on this young man's life. She glanced at Michael, seeing the same pride and emotion on his face.

However, as Tyler continued, sharing more details about his home life and his father's journey to recovery, Sarah noticed a shift in the room. Some parents were fidgeting uncomfortably, while others wore expressions of shock or disapproval.

Just as Tyler was wrapping up, a voice cut through the silence. "Is this really appropriate? Airing all this...dirty laundry in front of everyone?"

Sarah's heart sank as she recognized the speaker—Mrs. Anderson, one of the more conservative members of the church board. The woman's face was flushed with indignation as she continued, "And where were the proper authorities when all this was happening?"

The room erupted into murmurs, some agreeing with Mrs. Anderson, others coming to Tyler's defense. Sarah watched in horror as Tyler's face crumpled. The boy looked lost and betrayed.

Michael was already moving, placing a protective arm around Tyler's shoulders, and guiding him from the room. Sarah stepped forward as she tried to regain control of the situation.

"Everyone, please," she said, her voice steady despite her racing heart. "Tyler's bravery in sharing his story is commendable. It's important that we create a safe space for our youth to be honest about their struggles."

But the damage was done. As Sarah worked to calm the crowd and explain the importance of open dialogue, she could see the doubt and concern on many faces. What had started as a celebration of their ministry's impact had turned into a controversy that threatened to undermine everything they'd worked for.

As the event wound down, with many families leaving in a cloud of whispered conversations, Sarah felt a weight settling on her shoulders. She found Michael in the hallway; his expression grim as he filled her in on Tyler's state.

"He's devastated," Michael said. "Feels like he's let everyone down, exposed his family to judgment."

Sarah's heart ached for the teen. "We should have been better prepared for this," she said, frustration evident in her voice. "We should have known not everyone would understand."

Michael nodded, running a hand through his hair. "You're right. But Sarah, we can't let this setback discourage us. The fact that Tyler felt safe enough to share his story...that's a victory in itself."

As they stood there, the weight of the evening heavy between them, Pastor David approached. His expression was serious, his voice low as he said, "We have to talk. My office, first thing tomorrow morning."

Sarah and Michael exchanged a worried glance. They both knew that this conversation would be pivotal—not just for their ministry but also for their relationship.

They cleaned up the fellowship hall in somber silence. Sarah felt they were on the edge of a precipice. Their connection, their shared passion for their ministry—it all felt both incredibly precious and incredibly fragile in this moment.

"Michael," she said as they finished, "whatever happens tomorrow...we're in this together, right?"

He turned to her, his eyes filled with determination and tenderness that always made her breath catch. "Always," he said, pulling her into a gentle embrace. "No matter what, we face it together."

As Sarah drove home that night, her mind racing with the events of the evening and the uncertainty of what lay ahead, she clung to her faith more fiercely than ever. She prayed, her voice barely a whisper in the quiet of her car, "Lord, guide us through this storm. Help us to see Your purpose, even in these difficulties. And please...help us to be the support that Tyler and all these kids need right now."

The church parking lot was empty save for Michael's car, the silence broken by the distant hum of traffic. He sat behind the wheel, unable to bring himself to drive away, the events of the evening replaying in his mind like a relentless film reel.

His phone buzzed—a text from Tyler. *I'm sorry I messed everything up.*

Michael's heart clenched. *You didn't mess anything up, Tyler. You were brave. We'll get through this.*

As he hit send, Michael caught sight of his reflection in the rearview mirror. The man staring back at him looked tired and uncertain—a far cry from the confident youth pastor he strived to be.

"Lord," he whispered, "give me wisdom. Show me how to fix this."

Unable to face going home, he walked the quiet streets of the neighborhood. His feet carried him to the local park, where youth group activities were often held. The empty swing set creaked in the night breeze, a poignant reminder of the kids they were fighting for.

Sitting on a bench, Michael pulled out his Bible. It fell open to a familiar passage in James. "Consider it pure joy, my brothers and sisters, whenever you face trials of many kinds because you know that the testing of your faith produces perseverance."

Was this a test of their faith? Of their calling to ministry?

As he pondered this, a thought popped into his head. What if they could use this controversy to educate the congregation about the real issues facing their youth and foster greater understanding and support?

Energized by this new perspective, Michael began jotting down ideas on his phone. A community outreach program with workshops for parents, and testimonies from other youth who had overcome challenges.

His thoughts were interrupted by a text from Sarah. *I can't sleep. Keep thinking about Tyler and tomorrow's meeting. Are you okay?*

Michael smiled, feeling a wave of gratitude for her. *I'm working on some ideas. Would you like to meet me for breakfast before the meeting? We'll face this together.*

When he returned to his car, he felt a sense of purpose.

Driving home, he prayed, "Lord, thank You for this calling, for Sarah, for these kids who trust us. Guide us in the days to come. Help us to be the leaders and mentors they need."

He pulled into his driveway, exhausted but hopeful. Tomorrow would bring its own trials, but for tonight, he had faith that God was working even in this difficult situation.

He drifted to sleep. His dreams were filled with images of healed families, restored faith, and a thriving youth ministry. Through it all, Sarah's steady presence, her hand in his, guided them through this journey.

Michael's alarm blared, jolting him awake. As he reached to silence it, his eyes fell on the notepad by his bedside, filled with the thoughts he'd scribbled down in the park.

He'd slept well, wrapped in the peace of a faith that trusted God's plan, even when the path forward seemed uncertain.

Determined, he began to prepare for the day ahead, knowing their meeting with Pastor David could change many things.

Chapter 18

The morning sun filtered through the stained glass windows of Pastor David's office, casting colorful patterns across the worn carpet. Sarah sat rigid in her chair, acutely aware of Michael beside her. The silence in the room was heavy, broken only by the ticking of the old clock on the wall.

Pastor David leaned forward, his elbows resting on his desk. "I think we all know why we're here," he began, his voice grave. "Last night's...incident has raised serious concerns among the church leadership."

Sarah felt her heart sink. She glanced at Michael, and the determined set of his jaw helped. "Pastor," she said, fighting to keep her voice steady, "we understand that some people were uncomfortable with Tyler's testimony. But isn't it important that we create a space where our youth feel safe to share their struggles?"

Pastor David nodded. "Of course it is. But, Sarah, Michael...there are ways to do that without potentially exposing the church to liability issues. Some parents are questioning whether proper protocols were followed in reporting Tyler's situation."

Michael leaned forward, his voice earnest. "We followed all the proper channels, Pastor. We involved Child Protective Services. We supported Tyler's father in seeking treatment. Everything was done by the book."

"I believe you," Pastor David said, holding up a hand. "But perception is important. And right now, the perception is that our youth ministry might be...overstepping its bounds."

Sarah felt a flare of indignation. "Overstepping? By helping a child in need?"

Pastor David's expression softened. "I know your hearts are in the right place. But there's another issue we need to address." He paused, his gaze moving between them. "There's been talk about the nature of your relationship."

Sarah felt her cheeks flush. They'd been so careful to keep things professional at church. But clearly, their connection hadn't gone unnoticed.

Michael spoke up, his voice calm but firm. "Sarah and I are in a relationship, yes. But we've been careful not to let it interfere with our ministry duties."

Pastor David sighed, leaning back in his chair. "Under normal circumstances, I'd be thrilled for you both. But given the current situation...some board members feel it might be best if one of you stepped down from the youth ministry. At least temporarily."

The words hit Sarah deep in the pit of her stomach. She felt Michael stiffen beside her, his hand finding hers under the desk.

"Step down?" Sarah repeated, her voice barely a whisper. "But, Pastor, this ministry...it's our calling. We've seen such growth, such positive changes in these kids."

Pastor David's expression was sympathetic but firm. "I know. And believe me, I've argued on your behalf. But after last night...the board feels we need to take some time to reevaluate our youth program. To ensure we're operating within proper boundaries."

As the implications of his words sank in, Sarah felt anger at the injustice of it all. She feared for the future of their ministry, and felt an overwhelming sense of loyalty to the kids they'd come to care for.

She turned to Michael, seeing her own turmoil reflected in his eyes. They were facing a crossroads—not just in their ministry but also in their relationship.

"Can we have some time to discuss this?" Michael asked, his voice steady despite the tension Sarah could feel in his body.

Pastor David nodded. "Of course. Take the day to pray about it and consider your options. But I'll need a decision by tomorrow morning."

They left the office, and Sarah felt the ground shifting beneath her feet. The hallway seemed too bright and normal for the turmoil she felt inside.

"What are we going to do?" she asked once they were out of earshot.

Michael ran a hand through his hair, his expression troubled. "I don't know, Sarah. But we'll figure it out. Let's go somewhere we can talk."

They ended up at their spot in the park, where they'd had so many deep conversations about faith and ministry. As they sat on the familiar bench, Sarah felt desperation washing over her.

"I can't believe they're asking one of us to step down," she said, her voice choked with unshed tears. "After everything we've done, everything we've built..."

Michael pulled her close, his arm a comforting weight around her shoulders. "I know. It feels like we're being punished for following our calling, for trying to make a real difference in these kids' lives."

They discussed their options, weighing the pros and cons of each decision. Sarah instinctively felt they were being tested—not just by the church leadership but by God Himself.

"What if..." she began, "what if this is a sign? That we need to choose between our ministry and our relationship?"

Michael sat silent for a long moment, his gaze fixed on the distant horizon. When he spoke, his voice was soft but certain. "I don't believe that, Sarah. I can't believe God would ask us to choose between two things He's blessed us with—our calling to ministry and our love for each other."

Sarah felt her heart skip at the word "love." They hadn't said it out loud yet, but at that moment, she knew it was true. She loved Michael, not just for his passion for ministry but also for his faith, kindness, and strength.

"So what do we do?" she asked, looking up at him.

His gaze met hers, filled with a determination that made her breath catch. "We fight for what we believe in. We show them that our relationship strengthens our ministry, not weakens it. And we trust God has a plan, even if we can't see it right now."

They continued to talk, brainstorming ways to address the board's concerns while staying true to their calling. This setback, as difficult as it was, was an opportunity to demonstrate the depth of their commitment to everything.

By the time the sun began to set, painting the sky in brilliant hues of orange and pink, they had a plan. It wouldn't be easy, and there was no guarantee of success. But as Sarah looked at Michael, she saw the love and determination in his eyes.

They walked back to the church hand in hand, ready to draft the proposal they would present to Pastor David and the board in the morning. As they approached the building, Sarah caught sight of a familiar figure sitting on the steps.

Tyler looked up as they approached, his eyes red-rimmed but determined. "Ms. Thompson, Pastor Michael," he said, standing up. I...I wanted to apologize for causing all this trouble."

Sarah's heart ached for the young man. She stepped forward, placing a gentle hand on his shoulder. "Tyler, there is nothing to apologize for. You were incredibly brave in sharing your story."

Michael nodded in agreement. "Sometimes doing the right thing stirs up opposition. But that doesn't make it any less right."

Tyler looked between them, a flicker of hope crossing his face. "So...you're not giving up on the youth group? On us?"

Sarah exchanged a glance with Michael, feeling a surge of resolve. "Never," she said. "We're in this for the long haul, Tyler. No matter what obstacles on our path we face."

As they stood there in the gathering twilight, Sarah felt a sense of peace settling over her. Whatever the board decided tomorrow, she knew they were where they were meant to be—serving these kids, living out their faith, and facing each tough spot.

She sent a silent prayer of gratitude, "Thank you, Lord, for this calling. For these kids. For Michael. Guide us in the days ahead, and help us to be the leaders and mentors these young people need."

They bid Tyler good night and headed inside to work on their proposal. They were on the cusp of something big, she could feel it. It had its uncertainties, yes, but also an opportunity to prove that love, in all its forms, could be a powerful force for good in the world.

Sarah and Michael worked late into the night, their heads bent together over Michael's desk as they crafted their proposal.

The future was uncertain, but their shared purpose and faith gave them strength to face tomorrow. When Sarah headed home in the early morning hours, they both felt exhausted and exhilarated. The late morning would bring more issues, but for now, they'd take comfort in the knowledge that they're walking this path together.

The first rays of dawn peeked through the church windows as Michael saved the final draft of their proposal. He leaned back in his chair, his eyes burning from the hours of intense work. Sarah had left an hour ago, insisting on going home to change before the board meeting. The silence of the empty church pressed in on him, amplifying the gravity of what lay ahead.

A text alert broke the stillness. *Praying for you both.* It was from Tyler.

Michael's heart swelled with pride for the young man who had inadvertently sparked this crisis. He typed back a quick message of encouragement, then set his phone aside, his mind racing.

The proposal they'd crafted was solid, outlining a vision for the youth ministry that was both innovative and grounded in Scripture. But would it be enough to convince the board? And even if it was, how would they navigate the complexities of their personal relationship within the context of their professional roles?

His gaze fell on the framed photo on his desk—a younger version of Pastor David, his arm slung around the shoulders of a teenage boy—himself. The memory of his own tumultuous youth and the impact Pastor David had made on his life stirred something deep within him.

Seeking guidance, Michael pulled out his Bible. His gaze landed on a passage from 1 Corinthians: "Love never fails. But where there are prophecies, they will cease; where there are tongues, they will be stilled; where there is knowledge, it will pass away."

The words affirmed the path he and Sarah had chosen. Their love—for each other, the kids, and their ministry—was at the heart of everything they did. But with that realization came a new fear. What if the board couldn't see that? What if they viewed their relationship as a liability rather than a strength?

He knelt by his desk and offered a prayer. "Lord, guide us in this. Show us how to demonstrate that our love strengthens our ministry. And if this isn't Your will...give us the strength to accept a different path."

As he rose, Michael felt a sense of peace. Whatever the outcome of the meeting, he knew that he and Sarah were where God wanted them to be, doing what they were called to do.

The sound of the church door opening startled Michael from his thoughts. Sarah walked in, and came over to his office, her face a mix of determination and apprehension. "Ready?"

He nodded, reaching for her hand. "Together," he said, his voice steady despite the butterflies in his stomach.

They made their way to the boardroom. Michael's mind raced with last-minute preparations. But beneath the nervous energy was a bedrock of certainty.

They paused outside the boardroom door, the murmur of voices audible from within. Michael turned to Sarah, struck again by the depth of his feelings for her. "Whatever happens in there," he said, "I want you to know I love you. And I believe in us—in our ministry, relationship, and the work we're doing for these kids."

Sarah's eyes shone with unshed tears as she squeezed his hand. "I love you too," she whispered. "Let's do this."

As they entered the boardroom, heads turning to watch their entrance, Michael felt a surge of resolve. This wasn't just about defending their positions or their relationship. It was about fighting for the kids who needed them and for the ministry they believed in with all their hearts.

Chapter 19

The boardroom was silent as Sarah and Michael finished presenting their proposal. The tension in the air was palpable, and Sarah could feel her heart racing as she met the eyes of each board member. She glanced at Michael, his steady presence beside her was comforting.

Pastor David cleared his throat, breaking the silence. "Thank you both for this...comprehensive plan. You've clearly put a lot of thought into addressing our concerns."

Sarah nodded, her voice steady despite her nerves. "We believe in this ministry, Pastor. In these kids. We couldn't just walk away without fighting for what we've built."

One of the board members, Mrs. Anderson—the same woman who had objected to Tyler's testimony—leaned forward, her expression skeptical. "It all sounds very nice on paper, but how can we be sure you can maintain professional boundaries? Your...personal relationship complicates things."

Sarah felt a flare of indignation, but before she could respond, Michael spoke. "With all due respect, Mrs. Anderson, our relationship strengthens our ministry. Our shared faith, our commitment to these kids—it all works together."

Another board member, Mr. Johnson, nodded thoughtfully. "I can see that. But what about the liability issues? We can't have a repeat of the Tyler situation."

Sarah took a deep breath, steeling herself. "We understand your concerns. That's why we've proposed additional training for all youth leaders on proper reporting procedures. We've also included a plan for regular check-ins with a licensed counselor to ensure we're providing appropriate support to our kids."

As the discussion continued, with board members raising questions and concerns, Sarah felt hope and apprehension. They were listening and engaging with the proposal, but would it be enough?

After what felt like hours, Pastor David called for a vote. "All those in favor of accepting Sarah and Michael's proposal, allowing them to continue leading the youth ministry together, please raise your hands."

Sarah held her breath, her hand finding Michael's under the table. Time seemed to slow as she watched hands begin to rise. One, two, three...

In the end, the vote was close—6 to 5 in favor of their proposal. As Pastor David announced the result, Sarah felt relief. They had done it. They had fought for their ministry and won.

The meeting adjourned, and board members filed out, some offering congratulations, others still looking skeptical. Pastor David approached them, his expression one of pride and concern.

"You've been given a second chance," he said. "Don't waste it. Remember, a lot of eyes will be on you now. You'll need to be above reproach in everything you do."

Sarah nodded, feeling the weight of responsibility settling on her shoulders. "We understand, Pastor. Thank you for your support."

Stepping out into the bright sunlight, Sarah turned to Michael. "We did it," she said, her voice filled with wonder. "We really did it."

Michael pulled her into a tight embrace, his voice muffled against her hair. "We did. Together."

But as they stood there, basking in their victory, Sarah felt a nagging feeling of unease. Although they had won the battle, she sensed the war was far from over.

Her suspicions were confirmed later that evening as they met with the youth group to share the news. While many of the teens were excited about the continuation of their programs, Sarah noticed a few holding back, exchanging whispers and worried glances.

After the meeting, as they were cleaning up, Tyler approached them, his expression troubled. "Ms. Thompson, Pastor Michael...can we talk?"

Sarah's heart sank at the hesitation in his voice. "Of course, Tyler. What's on your mind?"

Tyler shuffled his feet, not meeting their eyes. "It's just...some of the kids are saying things. About you two, about the ministry. They're saying we can't trust you anymore, that you'll just report everything to the authorities."

Michael's face fell. "Tyler, you know that's not true. We only involve authorities when someone's safety is at risk."

Tyler nodded, but he still looked uncertain. "I know that. But...some of the others are talking about not coming back. They say it's not safe to share stuff anymore."

As Tyler walked away, Sarah felt the weight of their victory crumbling. She turned to Michael, seeing her own worry reflected in his eyes. "What have we done?" she whispered. "We fought so hard to keep the ministry going, but what if we've lost the kids' trust in the process?"

Michael pulled her close, his voice low. "We'll figure it out, Sarah. We've come too far to give up now."

As they locked up the church that night, Sarah couldn't shake the feeling that their greatest challenge was still ahead. They had won the board's approval, but now they faced an even more daunting task—rebuilding trust with the kids they had fought to serve.

She offered a silent prayer, her voice barely a whisper in the quiet night, "Lord, we need Your guidance now more than ever. Show us how to reach these kids and prove that our commitment to them is unwavering."

As they parted ways in the parking lot, Sarah felt pride in what they'd accomplished, but fear for the issues ahead. It felt rocky and uncertain. However, the overwhelming sense of love—for Michael, their ministry, and the kids they served—that was solid.

"We'll meet tomorrow," Michael said, squeezing her hand. "Start working on a plan to rebuild trust with the group."

Sarah nodded, forcing a smile. "Together," she said, echoing their earlier affirmation.

She drove home, her mind racing with ideas and worries, with the feeling they were on the verge of something monumental. That the coming days would test their faith, relationship, and commitment to their calling in ways they had never imagined.

But as she pulled into her driveway, a sense of peace settled over her. They would confront the problems as they had faced everything else. Together.

The digital clock on Michael's dashboard blinked—11:37 p.m. as he pulled into his driveway. He killed the engine but didn't move, the weight of the day's events pressing heavily on his shoulders. The board's approval should have felt like a victory, but Tyler's words echoed in his mind, a reminder of the fragile trust they'd worked so hard to build.

A text broke through his thoughts. It was from Jake, one of the teens. *Pastor M, is it true what they're saying? That you and Ms. Thompson are just looking out for yourselves now?*

Michael's heart felt heavy. He typed out a careful response, assuring Jake of their commitment to the youth group, but the doubt lingered. How had their relationship become a source of suspicion rather than strength?

Unable to face the emptiness of his apartment, he drove to the church. The building loomed dark and silent as he let himself in, muscle memory guiding him to the youth room.

Flicking on the lights, he was struck by the wall of photos—smiling faces of teens whose lives they'd touched. There was a picture of Tyler from the retreat. The boy's grin was carefree and open—so different from the guarded expression he'd worn tonight.

"Lord," Michael whispered into the quiet room, "where did we go wrong?"

Seeking guidance, he pulled out his Bible. 1 Corinthians. "If I speak in the tongues of men or angels, but do not have love, I am only a resounding gong or a clanging cymbal."

The words hit him like a physical blow. They'd been so focused on proving themselves to the board and defending their relationship that they'd lost sight of what mattered—showing God's love to these kids.

He once again sketched out a new plan—not just for rebuilding trust but for recommitting to their original calling. Ideas flowed—one-on-one mentoring sessions, a teen-led community service project, and an open forum for the youth to voice their concerns and shape the direction of the ministry.

The dawn light crept through the windows, and Michael felt exhausted but hopeful. They'd made mistakes, but it wasn't too late to make things right.

He pulled out his phone to text Sarah, then hesitated. Their relationship, beautiful as it was, had become a complicating factor. They needed to find a way to show the teens that their love strengthened their ministry rather than compromising it.

He typed, *Meet me at the church before youth group tonight. I think I know how we can fix this.*

Then drove home for a few hours of sleep.

Chapter 20

The youth room hummed with nervous energy as they prepared for the evening's meeting. It had been a week since they'd shared the news about the board's decision, and attendance had dwindled with each passing day. Sarah's stomach churned with anxiety as she arranged chairs in a circle, praying that tonight would be different.

As the teens began to trickle in, Sarah noticed the absence of several familiar faces. Tyler was there, along with Katie and a handful of others, but the room felt emptier than it had in months.

Michael cleared his throat, drawing everyone's attention. "Thanks for coming tonight, everyone. We know things have been...difficult lately. But we're here because we care about each and every one of you, and we want to rebuild the trust that's been shaken."

Sarah nodded, adding, "We've planned a special activity for tonight. Something to help us all reconnect and remember why we're here."

They explained the trust building exercise they'd devised. Sarah watched skepticism, hope, and lingering doubt play across their faces. She said a silent prayer, "Lord, help us reach them. Help us show them Your love."

The activity started with the kids participating half-heartedly. But as the evening wore on, Sarah began to see glimmers of the openness and vulnerability that had once characterized their group. Tyler, in particular, seemed to be thawing, his responses becoming more engaged and honest.

Just as Sarah was beginning to feel hope, the youth room door burst open. A woman Sarah recognized as Jake's mother stormed in, her face flushed with anger.

"Jake, we're leaving. Now," she demanded, her eyes flashing as they landed on Sarah and Michael. "I can't believe you're still running this...this mockery of a youth group."

Jake, who had been absent for the past week, shrunk in his chair. "Mom, please," he mumbled, embarrassed.

Sarah stepped forward, her heart racing. "Mrs. Williams, I understand you have concerns. Perhaps we could speak privately."

"I have nothing to say to you," Mrs. Williams snapped. "You claim to be helping these kids, but all you're doing is encouraging them to air their dirty laundry and turn against their families."

The room fell silent, the tension palpable. Sarah felt Michael beside her as he spoke up. "Mrs. Williams, that's not what we're doing here. We aim to provide a safe space for these young people to explore their faith and find support."

Mrs. Williams let out a harsh laugh. "Support? Is that what you call it when you report families to CPS? When you encourage kids to share private matters in public?"

Sarah's heart sank as she saw the other teens shifting from one foot to another, some avoiding eye contact. The trust they had been working so hard to rebuild was crumbling before her eyes.

"Mom, stop it," Jake said, his voice stronger now. He stood up, facing his mother. "Ms. Thompson and Pastor Michael have helped me a lot. They've never encouraged me to turn against you or Dad."

Mrs. Williams's face softened at her son's words, but her expression remained skeptical. "Jake, honey, I just don't want you getting mixed up in something that could hurt our family."

As the confrontation continued, Sarah felt proud of Jake for standing up for what he believed in, but feared this incident would drive away the few kids who had returned. Yet she also felt an overwhelming sense of determination to fight for their ministry.

After what felt like hours, Mrs. Williams agreed to a private meeting with Sarah, Michael, and Pastor David to discuss her concerns. As she left with Jake, the tension in the room began to dissipate.

Sarah turned to the remaining teens, her heart heavy. "I'm so sorry you all had to witness that. This is the kind of thing we want to avoid—making anyone feel unsafe or uncomfortable here."

To her surprise, it was Tyler who spoke up. "It's okay, Ms. Thompson. We know you and Pastor Michael are just trying to help. And...I think Jake standing up to his mom like that kind of proves it, you know?"

The small group murmured in agreement, and Sarah felt a glimmer of hope rekindling within her. She caught Michael's eye and saw her own mix of exhaustion and determination reflected there.

As they wrapped up the meeting, making plans for their next gathering, Sarah felt they were at a crucial turning point. The confrontation with Mrs. Williams had been painful, but it had also sparked a moment of solidarity among the remaining kids.

Later that night, as she and Michael sat in his office, going over plans for their meeting with the Williams, Sarah felt the weight of their calling more acutely than ever.

"Michael," she said, "are we doing the right thing? Fighting so hard to keep this ministry going, even when it seems like everything is working against us?"

He was quiet, his gaze thoughtful. Then he reached out, taking her hand in his. "Sarah, do you remember what first drew you to youth ministry?"

She nodded, a small smile playing on her lips. "The chance to make a real difference in these kids' lives. To show them God's love in a tangible way."

"Exactly," Michael said, squeezing her hand. "And that's still what we're doing, even if it looks different than expected. We're fighting for these kids, for their right to have a safe space to explore their faith and find support."

They continued to talk, thinking of ways to address Mrs. Williams's concerns while staying true to their calling. Difficult as it was, this was an opportunity to demonstrate the depth of their commitment.

When they decided to call it a night, they felt they'd accomplished something. They walked to their cars, and Sarah felt exhausted. Tomorrow would bring its own challenges, but for now, she took comfort in the knowledge they were walking this path together.

"Whatever happens in that meeting tomorrow," Michael said as they reached her car, "remember that we're in this together. You and me, partners in ministry and in life."

She felt her heart swell at his words, and leaned in to kiss him. "Together," she affirmed.

She drove home, the quiet streets contrasting with the upheaval of the evening. Sarah prayed for Michael's unwavering support, for the glimmers of hope they'd seen in the youth group, and for the strength to keep fighting for what they believed in.

She fell into bed, exhausted but determined. Sarah held onto the certainty that whatever came next, they would face it as they had faced everything else—a commitment to the calling God had placed on their lives.

After texting with Michael, she finally drifted to sleep, her mind full of plans and prayers for tomorrow.

As the first rays of sunlight began to filter through her curtains, she dreamed of a youth group restored, a ministry thriving, and a future bright with possibility—everything met and overcome through the power of faith and love.

The church parking lot had been empty as Michael locked up, the echo of his footsteps contrasting with the chaos of the evening's youth group meeting. He'd paused at his car, his gaze drawn to the illuminated cross atop the building. Its steady glow had seemed to mock the turmoil in his heart.

"Lord," he'd whispered, "are we on the right path?"

As if in answer, his phone had buzzed with a text from Tyler. *Thanks for tonight, Pastor M. It meant a lot that you guys didn't give up on us.*

Michael's heart had clenched, a mix of hope and worry washing over him. They were making progress, but at what cost? The confrontation with Mrs. Williams had shaken him more than he cared to admit.

Unable to face going home, he'd driven to the local park where he and Sarah often walked and talked. The empty playground equipment stood silent in the moonlight, a poignant reminder of the kids they were fighting for.

Sitting on a bench, he'd pulled out his Bible, turning to a familiar passage in Romans. "And we know that in all things God works for the good of those who love him, who have been called according to his purpose."

He'd read into the deeper meaning and wondered if the struggle was part of God's plan? A refining fire for their ministry and their relationship?

What if they could use this conflict as an opportunity to not just defend their ministry but transform it into something even more impactful?

Energized by this new perspective, he'd begun jotting down ideas on his phone. A parent-teen mentoring program, community service projects led by the youth, open forums for families to voice concerns and shape the ministry's direction...

His thoughts had been interrupted by a text from Sarah. *Can't sleep. Keep thinking about tomorrow's meeting. How are you doing?*

He'd smiled, feeling a wave of gratitude for her. "I'm working on some ideas. Would you like to meet me for breakfast before the meeting?"

As he'd driven home, he'd prayed. "Lord, thank You for this calling, for Sarah, for these kids who trust us. Guide us in the days to come. Help us to be the leaders and mentors they need."

He'd pulled into his driveway, exhausted but hopeful. He'd known the meeting with the Williams would be challenging, but for the first time in weeks, he'd felt a sense of clarity about their path forward.

He'd dreamed of healing families, restoring faith, and a thriving youth ministry. Through it all, Sarah was beside him, her hand in his as they navigated this journey.

Chapter 21

The Saturday morning sun streamed through the stained glass windows of Pastor David's office, casting a kaleidoscope of colors across the worn carpet. Sarah sat rigid in her chair, aware of Michael beside her and the palpable tension emanating from the Williams across the room. As Pastor David cleared his throat to begin the meeting, Sarah said a silent prayer, "Lord, guide our words and open hearts today."

"Thank you all for coming," Pastor David began, his voice calm and measured. "I understand there are concerns about our youth ministry that need to be addressed."

Mrs. Williams wasted no time in launching into her grievances. "Concerns? That's putting it mildly. These two," she gestured sharply at Sarah and Michael, "are encouraging our children to air private family matters and report their parents to authorities!"

Sarah felt her heart rate quicken, but before she could respond, Jake spoke up, his voice quiet but firm. "Mom, that's not true. Ms. Thompson and Pastor Michael have never encouraged me to do anything like that."

Mr. Williams, who had been silent until now, touched his wife's arm. "Let's hear them out, honey. There must be some misunderstanding here."

Michael leaned forward, his expression earnest. "Mr. and Mrs. Williams, I assure you our only goal is to provide a safe, supportive environment for our youth to explore their faith and grow as individuals."

"And what about Tyler?" Mrs. Williams countered. "Everyone knows you reported his family to CPS."

Sarah took a deep breath, steeling herself. "Mrs. Williams, I understand your concern. But we have a legal and moral obligation to report suspected abuse or neglect. In Tyler's case, his father was struggling with addiction, and Tyler himself asked for help."

The room fell silent for a moment, the weight of Sarah's words hanging in the air. Michael nodded and she knew he was there for her.

Pastor David spoke up, his voice gentle but firm. "Perhaps it would help if we clarified the policies and procedures of our youth ministry. Sarah, Michael, could you walk us through your approach?"

For the next hour, they outlined their ministry philosophy, reporting procedures, and commitment to supporting youth and their families. They shared stories of lives changed and teens finding hope and purpose through their faith.

As they spoke, Sarah noticed a gradual shift in the Wiliams' demeanor. The hostility in Mrs. Williams's eyes began to soften, replaced by a glimmer of understanding.

"I...I had no idea you were doing so much," she said, her voice quiet. "I just assumed..."

"We understand," Michael said. "It's natural to be protective of your children. We want to work with you, not against you, to support Jake and all our youth."

Mr. Williams nodded, a thoughtful expression on his face. "You mentioned family support programs. Could you tell us more about those?"

As the conversation turned to constructive discussions about parent involvement and family ministry, Sarah felt relief. They weren't out of the woods yet, but this was progress.

By the time the meeting concluded, a tentative peace had been reached. The Williams agreed to give the youth ministry another chance, even expressing interest in volunteering.

They all stood to leave. Mrs. Williams approached Sarah, her eyes shining with unshed tears. "I owe you an apology," she said. "I judged you without understanding. Can we...can we start over?"

Sarah felt her eyes welling up as she nodded, reaching to clasp Mrs. Williams's hand. "Of course. We're all on the same team here—Team Jake and Team Every-Kid-in-Our-Ministry."

After the Williams left, Sarah turned to Michael, exhausted but exhilarated. "Did that really just happen?" she asked, a disbelieving laugh bubbling up.

Michael pulled her into a tight embrace, his voice muffled against her hair. "It did. You were amazing, Sarah. Your passion, your commitment to these kids...it shone through every word."

As they stood there, basking in the aftermath of their hard-won victory, Pastor David approached, a warm smile on his face. "Well done, both of you. You've turned a potential crisis into an opportunity for growth and understanding."

Sarah felt a surge of gratitude, both for Pastor David's support and for the strength she and Michael had found in each other throughout this matter. "Thank you, Pastor. We couldn't have done it without your guidance."

As they left the office, stepping out into the bright afternoon sunlight, Sarah felt a sense of rightness. They had faced one of their biggest challenges yet and come out stronger for it.

"So," Michael said, a hint of mischief in his eyes, "ready to tackle the next crisis?"

Sarah laughed, linking her arm through his. "Bring it on. As long as we're facing it together."

But as they walked to their cars, discussing plans for the next youth group meeting, she couldn't shake the feeling that their greatest test was still to come. They had won over the Williams, but there were still skeptics on the church board, still teens who hadn't returned to the group.

She whispered a silent prayer, her voice low and hushed in the quiet parking lot, "Lord, thank You for this victory. Guide us as we move forward and help us always remember why we're doing this—to show Your love to these kids."

As she drove home, her mind racing with ideas for rebuilding and strengthening their ministry, Sarah felt joyful at the breakthrough with the Wiliams. It brought determination to keep fighting for their calling, and also an overwhelming sense of love—for Michael, their ministry, and the kids they served.

The setting sun had painted the church parking lot in hues of orange and gold as Michael had locked up the office. The events of the day—the meeting with the Williams, the breakthrough, the plans for moving forward—swirled in his mind.

As he reached his car, his phone buzzed with a notification. An email from an unfamiliar address caught his eye: National Youth Ministry Conference—Keynote Speaker Invitation.

Michael's heart raced as he skimmed the message. They wanted him and Sarah to share their experiences and speak about innovative approaches to youth ministry on a national stage. It was an incredible opportunity, a chance to impact thousands of young lives across the country.

But as the initial excitement faded, a knot formed in his stomach. Accepting would mean time away from their local ministry, just when they were rebuilding trust and momentum. And what about their relationship? How would it handle the added pressure and scrutiny?

Seeking guidance, he drove to he and Sarah's local park. Sitting on their favorite bench, he pulled out his much loved Bible, and let it fall open. "For my thoughts are not your thoughts, neither are your ways my ways," declares the Lord from Isaiah.

Was this invitation part of God's plan? A test of their commitment to their local ministry? Or an opportunity to expand their impact beyond anything they'd imagined?

He pondered this and began to pray, "Lord, give us wisdom. Show us how to balance our commitment to these kids with the chance to reach a wider audience. And if this is Your will, help us navigate it in a way that honors You and strengthens our ministry—and our relationship."

His thoughts were interrupted by a text from Sarah. *Just got the conference invite. My mind is racing. Can we talk?*

Michael smiled, feeling grateful for her. *Meet me at our bench in the park. We'll figure this out together.*

He felt excited at the possibilities this opportunity presented. But also, some apprehension about the situations it might bring. It was a lot all at once.

He saw Sarah approaching, her face a mirror of his own conflicted emotions, and felt an overwhelming sense of love and respect for the woman who had become not just his partner in ministry but in life. As she sat beside him, he took her hand, marveling at how natural it felt.

"So," he said, "looks like God might be opening a new door for us."

Sarah nodded, squeezing his hand. "It's an amazing opportunity. But Michael, what about our kids here? We've just started to rebuild their trust."

He felt a surge of pride for Sarah's dedication. "I know. That's what we need to figure out. How do we balance this local ministry we've poured our hearts into with the chance to impact youth on a national scale?"

They began to discuss the pros and cons, devising ways to potentially do both. He knew that whatever they decided, God would guide them.

Chapter 22

The youth room buzzed with an energy Sarah hadn't felt in weeks. Teens chatted as they entered, some arriving early to help set up. As Sarah arranged chairs in a circle, she caught Michael's eye across the room, sharing a smile that spoke volumes about their hope.

Just as they were about to begin, the door burst open, and Tyler rushed in, his face flushed with excitement. "Ms. Thompson, Pastor Michael, you'll never guess what happened!"

Sarah's heart leaped, thrilled at Tyler's enthusiasm but wary of what news could have him so worked up. "What is it, Tyler?"

"My dad," he said, his words tumbling out in a rush. "He's been sober for three months and got a job! A real, steady job!"

The room erupted in cheers and congratulations. Sarah felt tears pricking at her eyes as she hugged Tyler, overwhelmed by the tangible proof of the difference their ministry was making.

As the meeting got underway, she loved the change in atmosphere. The trust-building exercises they had planned flowed, with teens opening up about their struggles and victories in a way they hadn't in months.

Halfway through the evening, Jake raised his hand, his expression serious. "I...I want to apologize," he said, his voice steady despite the emotion in his eyes. "For doubting you guys, for not standing up sooner when my mom said all that stuff. You've always been there for us, and I should have had your back."

Sarah felt her heart swell with pride and love for these incredible young people. She glanced at Michael, seeing her own feelings reflected in his eyes.

"Jake," Michael said, "there's nothing to apologize for. We're just grateful to have you back with us—all of you," he added, his gaze sweeping the room. "This group, this ministry—it's not about us. It's about creating a space to grow in your faith and support each other."

As the meeting wound down, Sarah felt a sense of peace. They had weathered the storm, and their ministry was emerging stronger for it.

But as the last of the teens filed out, still chatting and laughing, Pastor David appeared in the doorway, his expression unreadable. "Sarah, Michael, can I see you both in my office? There's something we need to discuss."

Sarah glanced at Michael as they followed Pastor David down the hallway. After all they'd been through, what could possibly be coming next?

As they settled into the familiar chairs in his office, Sarah's mind raced. Had there been more complaints? Was the board reconsidering their decision?

Pastor David leaned forward; his hands clasped on his desk. "First of all, I want to commend you both on the incredible work you've done rebuilding trust with our youth and their families. The transformation has been remarkable."

Sarah felt a flutter of hope inside her. "Thank you, Pastor. It hasn't been easy, but seeing the kids tonight...it makes it all worth it."

Michael nodded in agreement. "We feel blessed to be part of this ministry."

Pastor David smiled, but there was a hint of something in his eyes—sadness, resignation? "That's actually what I wanted to talk to you about. I received a call today from the director of a national youth ministry organization. They've been following the work you've been doing here, and...well, they want to offer you both positions."

Sarah felt as though the air had been sucked out of the room. She turned to Michael, seeing her own shock mirrored in his expression.

"Positions?" Michael managed to ask. "What kind of positions?"

Pastor David took a deep breath. "They want you to head up a new initiative, developing youth ministry programs for churches across the country. It's...well, it's an incredible opportunity. The chance to impact thousands of young lives."

Sarah's mind whirled with the implications. A national platform for their ministry, the ability to shape youth programs on a grand scale...it was beyond anything she had ever imagined.

But as she looked around the familiar office, thought of the teens they had just left—Tyler with his incredible news, Jake with his heartfelt apology—she felt a pang in her chest.

"This is...wow," she said, her voice barely a whisper. "I don't know what to say."

Michael reached for her hand, his touch grounding her in the moment. "It's a lot to process," he said, his voice steady despite the emotion she could see in his eyes. "How long do we have to make a decision?"

Pastor David sighed. "They're eager to move forward. They've asked for an answer within the week."

As they left the office a short while later, armed with information packets and contact details, Sarah felt like she was walking in a daze. The opportunity before them was incredible, a chance to expand their ministry beyond anything they had dreamed.

But as they reached the youth room, now quiet and empty, Sarah felt a lump forming in her throat. This room, these kids—this was where their hearts were. Could they really leave it all behind?

Michael pulled her close, seeming to read her thoughts. "We don't have to decide anything tonight," he said, cupping her cheek. "Let's take some time to pray about it, to really consider what God is calling us to do."

Sarah nodded, grateful for his solid presence. "You're right. This is...it's too big to rush into."

They locked up the church and walked to their cars, Sarah feeling they were on the edge of something monumental. The decision before them would shape not just their ministry but their entire lives.

She offered a prayer, her voice a whisper in the quiet night, "Lord, we need Your guidance now more than ever. Show us the path You want us to take, whether here or somewhere new."

As she drove home, her mind was making her giddy as she felt the weight of the decision before her. It wasn't just about their ministry anymore—it was about their relationship, their future together.

She thought of the kids they had just left; of the progress they had made in rebuilding trust. Could they really walk away now, just when things were getting back on track?

But then she thought of the potential impact they could have on a national scale; of the thousands of young lives they could touch. Wasn't that what their calling was all about—reaching as many kids as possible with God's love?

She pulled into her driveway. Her phone buzzed with a text from Michael. *Can't stop thinking about everything. Breakfast tomorrow to talk it through?*

Sarah smiled, feeling a wave of gratitude for him. *Absolutely. 7 o'clock at The Cozy Corner?*

His response came immediately. *It's a date. Love you.*

As she got ready for bed, Sarah's gaze fell on a familiar passage. "For I know the plans I have for you," declares the Lord, "plans to prosper you and not to harm you, plans to give you hope and a future." (Jeremiah 29:11)

She traced the words with her finger, feeling a sense of peace. Whatever decision they made, whatever path they chose, she knew that God would be with them every step of the way.

She slept, held in the arms of a love that was bigger than any decision, any ministry, any future she could imagine. Her dreams filled with images of smiling teens, Michael by her side, and ministry opportunities stretching out before them like an endless horizon. Through it all, a sense of purpose and calling transcended any single place or program.

The digital clock on Michael's nightstand blinked at 3:17 a.m., but sleep eluded him. His mind raced with the events of the day—the joy of Tyler's news, the renewed energy in the youth group, and the unexpected offer that now loomed before them. He sat up, reaching for his Bible on the bedside table.

As he flipped through the pages, a small photo fluttered out—a snapshot of him and Sarah at the youth retreat, surrounded by smiling teens. The image tugged at his heart, a reminder of what they'd be leaving behind if they accepted the national position.

"Lord," he whispered into the darkness, "is this really Your plan for us?"

Seeking guidance, the page opened on a passage from Isaiah. "For my thoughts are not your thoughts, neither are your ways my ways," declares the Lord. "As the heavens are higher than the earth, so are my ways higher than your ways and my thoughts than your thoughts."

The words called to him. Was this offer a divine calling to a larger mission? Or a test of their commitment to the local ministry they'd poured their hearts into?

Unable to find rest, he slipped out of bed and went to his study to make notes. Ways they might be able to balance a national role with their local responsibilities, potential successors who could carry on their work in Oakbrook, and strategies for maintaining connections with their current youth group even from afar.

As he worked, a new perspective began to form. What if this wasn't an either-or decision? What if God called them to expand their impact while honoring their local commitments?

Energized by this thought, Michael started outlining a proposal. They could take on the national role part-time, developing resources and training programs that could benefit youth ministries nationwide. Meanwhile, they could restructure their local program, empowering other leaders in the church to take on more responsibility while still maintaining their presence and influence.

Michael felt a sense of peace. They still had much to discuss and many details to work out, but he felt confident they were on the right track.

He crawled back into bed for a few hours of sleep and offered a prayer of gratitude for everything he was being given.

Chapter 23

The Cozy Corner Café buzzed with the Sunday morning crowd, the aroma of freshly brewed coffee filling the air. Sarah sat at their usual table, her fingers tracing the rim of her mug as she waited for Michael. Her mind raced with the implications of the decision before them—a national platform for their ministry or staying with the local youth group they'd put everything into.

Michael walked in, their eyes met, and Sarah felt a flutter in her stomach that had nothing to do with nerves. Even after everything they'd been through, his presence still had the power to calm her racing thoughts.

"Hey," he said, sliding into the seat across from her, reaching for her hand and giving it a squeeze. "Did you get any sleep last night?"

Sarah shook her head, managing a wry smile. "Not much. You?"

He let go of her hand and ran his fingers through his hair, his expression mirroring her own mix of excitement and apprehension. "Same. I kept thinking about the kids, the opportunity...about us."

As they discussed the pros and cons of taking the national position, Sarah felt good about how in sync they were, anticipating each other's thoughts and concerns.

"It's an incredible opportunity," Michael said, his eyes alight with possibility. "Think of how many young lives we could impact on a national scale."

Sarah nodded, feeling a surge of excitement at the thought. "And the resources we'd have access to, the ability to shape youth ministry programs across the country..."

But even as the words left her mouth, she felt a pang in her chest. She thought of Tyler's beaming face as he shared his father's success, Jake's heartfelt apology, and the new girl Katie's shy smile as she began to open up in group discussions.

"But?" Michael prompted, correctly reading the conflict in her eyes.

She took a deep breath. "But...these kids, Michael. Our kids. We've been through so much with them. Can we really walk away when things are getting back on track?"

He reached across the table, taking her hand in his. "I know. I feel it too. The connection we have with this group, the trust we've rebuilt...it's special."

As they weighed the impact they could have nationally against the deep, personal connections they'd forged locally, Sarah felt the weight of the decision pressing down on her.

"What if..." she said, "what if we didn't have to choose? What if there was a way to do both?"

Michael's eyebrows rose, and he smiled. "What are you thinking?"

Sarah leaned forward, her words coming faster as the concept took shape. "What if we proposed a modified role? We could take on the national position part-time, developing programs and resources, but still maintain our local ministry here?"

Michael loved this woman so much. It was amazing how in sync they were. He didn't have the heart to tell her he'd thought the same thing last night and had spent the night drawing up a proposal. It was more fun to do it together with Sarah anyway.

As they fleshed out the idea, she felt a spark of hope in her chest. It wouldn't be easy—balancing national responsibilities with their local commitment would be challenging—but it felt right.

"We'd need to talk to Pastor David," Michael said, his expression thoughtful. "And, the national organization would have to agree to a modified role."

Sarah nodded, feeling a mix of excitement and nervousness. "It's a long shot, but...I think it's worth trying. It feels like a way to honor our calling to these specific kids and the opportunity to impact youth ministry on a larger scale."

As they finished their coffee and prepared to head to the church to speak with Pastor David before services started for the day, Sarah felt a sense of peace. Whatever the outcome, she knew they were facing this decision, united in their faith and commitment to their ministry.

David was in his office, poring over some paperwork. He looked up as they entered, a knowing smile crossing his face. "I had a feeling I'd be seeing you two early this morning. Have you made a decision?"

Sarah and Michael exchanged a glance before Michael spoke. "We have an idea we'd like to run by you, Pastor."

As they outlined their proposal for a hybrid role—part national, part local—Sarah watched Pastor David's expression. She saw surprise, thoughtfulness, and, finally, a glimmer of approval.

"It's an ambitious plan," he said. "Balancing national responsibilities with your commitment here won't be easy. But," he added, a smile spreading across his face, "I think it's brilliant. It's a way to expand your impact without abandoning the personal connections you've built here."

Sarah felt a wave of relief. "So you think it could work?"

He nodded. "I do. It will take some negotiation with the national organization, and we'll need to adjust some things here at the church. But if anyone can make it work, it's you two."

As they left his office, armed with his blessing and a plan to contact the national organization, Sarah felt excitement but also some trepidation. They had a direction now, a vision for their future, but there were still hurdles to overcome.

"What now?" she asked, turning to Michael.

He smiled, pulling her close. "Now, we pray. We make our proposal to the national organization. And," he added, his voice softening, "we talk to the kids. They deserve to hear this from us first."

Sarah nodded, feeling a lump in her throat at the thought of breaking the news to their youth group. "You're right. Whatever happens with the national position, they need to know that they're still our priority."

The sun had long since set, but Michael still sat at his desk in the church office, poring over the details of their proposal for the national organization. The excitement of their new plan mingled with a nagging worry in his gut. He glanced at the clock—8:37 p.m. In less than twenty-four hours, they'd share their decision with the youth group.

A soft knock at the door startled him. Tyler stood in the doorway. His face held concern and determination. "Pastor Michael? Can we talk?"

Michael's heart raced. Had Tyler overheard their plans? "Of course, Tyler. Come in."

As Tyler settled into the chair across from him, Michael said a silent prayer, "Lord, guide my words."

"I heard you and Ms. Thompson talking earlier," Tyler began, his voice quiet as a breath. "About some national thing. Are you...are you leaving us?"

The pain in Tyler's voice hit Michael like a punch in the gut. This was the challenge they'd feared—how to expand their ministry without the kids feeling abandoned.

Taking a deep breath, he leaned forward. "Tyler, I want you to know that no matter what opportunities come our way, you—all of you kids—are our priority. We're not leaving. We're just...exploring ways to help even more young people while still being here for you."

As he explained their hybrid plan, Michael watched Tyler's expression. He saw confusion, then a glimmer of understanding, and something that looked like pride.

"So," Tyler said, "you'd be helping other youth groups be more like ours? Teaching other leaders to do what you and Ms. Thompson do?"

Michael nodded, feeling hope. "That's the idea. But we can't do it without your support and the support of others. We'll need your help to make this work."

Tyler sat up straighter, a new light in his eyes. "Maybe...maybe we could help? Like, share our stories with other groups or something?"

As they continued to talk, inventing ways for the youth group to be involved in the national initiative, Michael felt a renewed direction in his calling. This wasn't just about him and Sarah anymore—it was about empowering these kids to be part of something bigger than themselves.

When Tyler left, promising to keep their conversation confidential until the official announcement, Michael said a prayer of gratitude, "Thank You, Lord, for using Tyler to show us the way forward."

He reached for his phone and typed a quick message to Sarah. *Had an unexpected visitor. I think we've found our angle for tomorrow's meeting. Call you in the morning.*

He locked up the church and headed home. Michael's mind was awash with new possibilities. The path ahead would be challenging, balancing their local commitments with national responsibilities. But with the kids involved, supporting and growing alongside them, it felt right.

Chapter 24

As they walked hand in hand to the youth room to prepare for that evening's meeting, Sarah said a silent prayer of gratitude for Michael's support, Pastor David's guidance, and the clarity they'd found in this moment of decision.

As they reached the youth room door, Michael squeezed her hand. "Ready for this?"

Sarah took a deep breath. "Ready," she affirmed. "Whatever happens, we're in this together."

With that, they stepped into the room, prepared to face whatever lay ahead in the exciting but uncertain future stretching out before them.

The youth room fell silent as they finished explaining their potential new role and the decision they faced. The teens' faces were a mix of surprise, confusion, and, in some cases, fear.

Jake was the first to speak, his voice gentle and faint. "So...you're leaving us?"

Sarah felt her heart clench at the pain in his voice. "No, Jake," she said. "That's why we wanted to talk to you all first. We're considering a way to balance our work here with a national role. But nothing is decided yet, and your thoughts and feelings are a huge part of our decision."

Michael nodded, "We want you to know that no matter what happens, you are our priority. This group, this ministry—it's not just a job for us. It's a calling."

As the teens began to voice their thoughts and concerns, Sarah and Michael listened. Some, like Katie, expressed excitement about the potential impact they could have on a national scale. Others, like Jake, worried about how things might change in the local group.

"But who would lead the group while you're doing national stuff?" Tyler asked, his brow furrowed.

It was a valid question, one that Sarah and Michael had discussed at length. "We've talked to Pastor David about training additional youth leaders," Michael explained. "People who share our vision and can support the group when we're focused on national projects."

As the discussion continued, Sarah marveled at the maturity and insight of these young people. They asked thoughtful questions, offered suggestions, and even proposed ways they could support the expanded ministry.

Halfway through the meeting, Esme—one of the quieter members of the group—raised her hand. "I have a question," she said, her voice soft but steady. "If you take this national role, even part-time...will you still have time for our individual stuff?"

The room fell silent, all eyes turning to Sarah and Michael. Sarah felt a lump form in her throat, touched by the vulnerability in Esme's question and the clear need for reassurance from the group.

"Esme," Sarah said, moving to kneel beside the girl's chair, "I want you to know that no matter what role we're in, no matter how busy things get, we will always, always make time for you. For each and every one of you."

Michael nodded in agreement. "Your individual journeys, your personal growth, and challenges—that's the heart of our ministry. No national program or resource we develop could be more important than our relationships with each of you."

They continued to address the kids' concerns and questions, and Sarah felt a shift in the room's energy. The initial fear and uncertainty gave way to cautious excitement and a sense of being part of something bigger.

Tyler, quiet since his initial question, spoke up again. "You should do it," he said, his voice growing stronger as he continued. "What you've done for me, for all of us...other kids deserve that too. And maybe, if you're developing programs for other churches, you can make sure they know how to handle situations like mine. So other kids don't have to go through what I did alone."

Sarah felt tears pricking at her eyes, overwhelmed by Tyler's growth and insight. She glanced at Michael, seeing her own emotion reflected in his eyes.

As the meeting drew to a close, they were surrounded by teens who offered hugs, words of encouragement, and promises to support the expanded ministry in any way they could.

"We'll help train the new leaders," Jake offered.

"And we can do fundraisers to support your travel for the national stuff," Katie added.

Sarah felt her heart swell with pride and love for these incredible young people. They had faced this potential change not with resistance but with maturity and a desire to be part of the solution.

As the last of the teens filed out, still chatting about ways to support the new ministry direction, Sarah turned to Michael. "That went so much better than I ever could have imagined," she said, her voice thick with emotion.

Michael pulled her into a tight embrace. "It did. These kids never cease to amaze me. Their faith, resilience, and capacity for growth—it's incredible."

As they stood in the now quiet youth room, Sarah felt a sense of peace. The path ahead was still uncertain, with many details to work out and things to face. But at this moment, she felt more certain than ever that they were moving in the right direction.

"So," Michael said, pulling back to meet her eyes, "are we doing this? Taking the leap into this new chapter?"

Sarah took a deep breath, feeling excited with nervous anticipation. "I think we are. Balancing everything won't be easy, but...I believe this is where God is leading us. And after tonight, seeing how the kids responded, I feel like we have an army of support behind us."

Michael's face broke into a wide grin. "We do. And we have each other. Partners in ministry and in life, remember?"

"Partners," she agreed, reaching up to kiss him, her heart skipping a beat.

They left the church that night, walking hand in hand to their cars. Sarah reflected on the journey that had brought them to this point. The challenges they'd faced, the growth they'd experienced, the lives they'd touched—it all seemed to be culminating in this new opportunity.

She offered a silent prayer of gratitude, "Thank You, Lord, for this calling. For these amazing kids. For Michael. Guide us as we step into this new chapter, and help us always remember why we're doing this—to show Your love to as many young people as we can reach."

As they parted ways, with plans to meet early the next morning to go over their draft proposal for the national organization, Sarah felt a sense of anticipation building inside her. The future stretched out before them, full of possibilities and struggles.

She fell asleep that night, her dreams filled with visions of youth groups across the country, of lives transformed by God's love.

Epilogue

The soft glow of the laptop screen illuminated Michael's face as he put the finishing touches on their first national youth ministry webinar. It was just after 2:30 a.m. in the morning, but the excitement of their new venture kept him wide awake. As he saved the file, a notification popped up—an email from a youth pastor in California seeking advice on a sensitive situation with one of his teens.

Michael's heart raced as he read the details. It was eerily similar to what they'd faced with Tyler months ago. This was why they'd taken on the national role, but now, faced with the reality of it, he felt the weight of responsibility settling on his shoulders.

"Lord," he whispered into the quiet room, "give me wisdom to guide this pastor, to help this child I've never met."

As he began to type his response, his mind drifted to their local youth group. They had a meeting tomorrow night—or rather, tonight—and he realized with a pang of guilt that he hadn't finished preparing for it. How could they balance these growing national responsibilities with their commitment to their local kids?

Seeking guidance, Michael let his Bible fall open. 1 Corinthians. "To the weak I became weak, to win the weak. I have become all things to all people so that by all possible means, I might save some."

Yes. Wasn't this expanded ministry a way of becoming "all things to all people"? But it also served as a reminder—they couldn't lose sight of the individual in their quest to reach the many.

Michael turned back to his computer. He finished his email to the California pastor, offering support and resources, then immediately opened his notes for the local youth group meeting. As he worked, he wondered, what if they involved the local teens in responding to some of these national inquiries? It could be a powerful learning experience for them, a way to expand their own understanding and empathy.

As four o'clock rolled around, Michael felt a mix of exhaustion and exhilaration. The path ahead was trying, but he felt more certain than ever that they were where God wanted them to be.

He reached for his phone to text Sarah, then hesitated, realizing the late hour. Instead, he typed an email outlining his idea for involving the local youth in their national work. As he hit send, he felt his usual surge of love and gratitude for his partner in all of this.

Crawling into bed, Michael offered a prayer of thanks for the opportunities before them, for the lives they were touching both near and far, and for the incredible journey they were on.

He drifted off to sleep, holding onto the peace that came from knowing they were walking in God's will, impacting lives across the nation while staying rooted in the community that had shaped them.

When his alarm blared, he reached to silence it, and he gazed at a framed photo of their youth group. He was tired but with determination he began to prepare for another full day of local ministry and national impact.

The obstacles were many, but as he got ready, he felt a sense of purpose and joy.

The gentle hum of the coffee maker had filled Sarah's kitchen as she poured over the latest email from the national youth ministry organization. She'd already been up for hours, unable to sleep with the weight of their new responsibilities on her mind. The email detailed their first assignment—a struggling youth group in a small town, desperate for guidance.

Sarah's heart raced as she read the details. This was the kind of impact they'd hoped to have, but now, faced with the reality, she felt a twinge of doubt. How could they help a group they'd never met hundreds of miles away?

"Lord," she whispered, clutching her coffee mug, "are we really equipped for this?"

As she contemplated their approach, her phone buzzed with a text from Katie. *Ms. Thompson, can we talk before school? It's important.*

Sarah's stomach clenched. They had a local youth group meeting tonight, and she realized with a pang of guilt that she hadn't given it much thought, so focused on their national work. They needed to find a balance with these growing responsibilities without neglecting the kids who supported their new venture.

Seeking guidance, she reached for her Bible and a passage from Matthew. "Therefore, go and make disciples of all nations, baptizing them in the name of the Father and of the Son and of the Holy Spirit, and teaching them to obey everything I have commanded you. And surely, I am with you always, to the very end of the age."

The words renewed her energy and reminded her of their true purpose—to share God's love and teachings, both near and far. But they also served as a gentle nudge—they couldn't forget the "nations" in their own backyard.

Opening Michael's email, she grinned. They were in sync as always with their ideas. She began drafting an email to the struggling youth group while jotting down ideas for that evening's local meeting. As she worked, an idea sparked. What if they involved their local teens in creating solutions for the distant group? It could be a great learning experience, broadening their perspective and deepening their faith.

As the sun began to rise, Sarah felt tired but also excited. The path ahead was daunting, but she felt more certain than ever that they were walking in God's will.

She reached for her phone, eager to call Michael and share her idea. As it rang, she felt a surge of love and gratitude for her partner in ministry and life.

"Michael," she said as soon as he answered, feeling herself brimming with enthusiasm, "I think I know how we can make this work. It's all about integration..."

As she outlined her plan, Sarah felt that although there were many hurdles, with faith, creativity, and commitment to both their local and national calling, they could navigate this new chapter together.

About the Author

Sandra E. Sinclair

Sandra E. Sinclair is a dreamer and hopeless romantic. She grew up in London, England where the skies are often gray, and the streets could be cleaner. However, she doesn't let this dampen her spirits. She loves her hometown and considers herself a true-blue Londoner, who is happy to find her sunshine overseas, and she does as often as she can. It's through traveling abroad that she finds her inspiration for her stories.

http://read.sandraesinclair.com

Other Books by Sandra E. Sinclair

Christian Romance

A Test of Faith

Prequel

Vignette

Book 1

Don't miss out!

Visit the website below and you can sign up to receive emails whenever Sandra E Sinclair publishes a new book. There's no charge and no obligation.

https://books2read.com/r/B-A-YEBD-UIPHE

Also by Sandra E Sinclair

Catica Island Inspired Romance
Island Promise
Island Bound
Island Rapture
Island Pearl

Locket of Love Series
Disarming Amy
Honoring Faith

Oakbrook
A Test of Faith

Oakbrook Faithful Heart
Pastor's Heart

Sweethearts of Jubilee Springs

Hope Eternal
Minding Benji
Blind Affection
Gambled Pride
Captured Heart

The Unbridled Series
Lost Fortune
Wild Storm
Love Letters
Calm Surrender

Timeless Hearts Series
Timeless Whisper
Timeless Storm
Timeless Pleasure